OTHER BOOKS by KASSANDRA LAMB

The Kate Huntington Mysteries

Psychotherapist Kate Huntington helps others cope with trauma, but she has led a charmed life...until a killer rips it apart. (10 novels)

The Kate on Vacation Mysteries

Even on vacation, Kate Huntington can't stay out of trouble. (4 novellas)

The Marcia Banks and Buddy Cozy Mysteries

Marcia Banks trains service dogs for veterans, and solves crimes on the side, with the help of her Black Lab, Buddy. (13 novels/novellas)

The C.o.P. on the Scene Mysteries

Eight days into her new job as Chief of Police in a small Florida city, Judith Anderson finds herself one step behind a serial killer. (spinoff from the Kate Huntington series; 2 novels–more to come)

Romantic Suspense

written under the pen name of Jessica Dale

AULD LANG MAYFAIR

A Marcia Banks and Buddy Mystery

Kassandra Lamb

author of the Kate Huntington Mysteries

a *misterio press* publication

Published by *misterio press LLC*

Cover art by Melinda VanLone, Book Cover Corner
Photo credits: silhouette of woman and dog © Majivecka (right to use
purchased through dreamstime.com)

Auld Lang Mayfair is a work of fiction. All names, characters, events and
most places are products of the author's imagination. Any resemblance to
actual events or people, living or dead, is entirely coincidental. Some real
places may be used fictitiously. Crystal County and the town of Mayfair,
Florida are fictitious.

ISBN: 978-1-947287-43-3

CHAPTER ONE

The baby balanced precariously on a stack of throw pillows at one end of the loveseat. She reached for the top shelf of the bookcase, where various tantalizing breakables resided.

Buddy watched from below, his gray-flecked snout twitching with anxiety.

I raced across the study, almost tripping over the puppy, who'd chosen that moment to master cocking his back leg in the air to pee. Unfortunately, he was peeing on the leg of my desk.

Meanwhile, my laptop beeped with an incoming email and my phone shrilled out Will's ringtone. Welcome to my world of multitasking, aka motherhood.

I dove for Noelle, plucking her off her pillowy mountain. "It's okay, Buddy," I reassured my Black Lab/Rottie.

I lowered the just turned one-year-old into her mesh-sided play yard in the corner, then grabbed my phone off the desk. Of course, the call had already gone to voicemail.

With phone pinched between ear and shoulder, I wiped up the puppy's mess. "Hey," Will said in his message, "I'm thinking I'm going to pack this in soon. It's almost dark and I doubt this guy's going to do anything tonight, not in this rain. And we've got a lot to do to get ready for Christmas."

So true. Day after tomorrow, my brother and his family would be arriving to inhabit our guest suite until December 26th.

Sounds good, I texted back and picked up the puppy.

He was also a Black Labrador—still officially unnamed, although I'd begun to think of him as Boo-Boo. We probably should've waited until Noelle was older to take on a puppy. But I was hoping to eventually train this little guy as a replacement mentor dog. Buddy was due for retirement from the task of helping me train my service dogs.

"If you don't pick up on this house-training thing soon," I told the pup, "I might start calling you Poo-Poo." He licked my chin.

Buddy whined, and I looked up. Noelle was once again climbing out of her play yard. She expertly dropped to her hands and knees and crawled toward the loveseat.

I sighed, putting the puppy down to scoop up the baby instead. With her propped on one side—I'd finally found a good use for my more than ample hips—I walked into the living room. She ran her little fingers through my long auburn ponytail.

I pointed out the picture window at the barn across the street, barely visible through sheets of rain—a northern cold front had collided with warmer, moister air from the south right over central Florida. Fortunately, Susanna Mayfair, my "co-manager" of the boarding stable, had been able to get the horses into their stalls before the storm hit.

"That's where our horse lives," I told Noelle. "Can you say her name, Niña?"

"Nee-yee," she mimicked.

"Close enough. How about Ma-ma?"

"Nee-yee," she said again, her blue eyes—so like Will's—sparkling at me.

I shook my head, even as my heart swelled in my chest. She might not be calling me *Mama* yet, but I loved this little creature beyond imagination.

I glanced up. The rain had let up some. Beyond the barn, along the road coming into town, I could make out the row of new shops that Susanna's octogenarian aunt had contracted to have built. As matriarch of the town her brother originally founded, Edna Mayfair was constantly searching for ways to bolster its economy. This was her latest endeavor—eight attached buildings, designed to be gift shops and such, with a quaint boardwalk along their front, inviting tourists to check them out.

Praying they would be a success, I headed back into the study. The baby still on my hip, I grabbed two throw pillows to add to the pile of off-limits-to-Noelle items in one corner of the master bedroom. *Heaven help us when this child figures out how to turn doorknobs!*

A brisk knocking on the front door.

What the…? Who would come calling in this downpour? I dropped the pillows back on the loveseat and hustled to the living room to look out the window again.

Carla Cummings stood on the front porch, hairnet plastered to her head, water streaming down her face. Her soaked apron, with Mayfair Diner on the bib, clung to her angular frame.

I yanked open the door.

"Sorry," she yelled over the splattering of the rain on the sidewalk behind her. "But I had to get out of there, before I killed him!"

⊷———⊶

"Him" turned out to be Carla's ex-husband. He'd shown up at the Mayfair Diner just as Carla, the dinner-shift manager, was relieving Jess Randall, the diner's owner.

He had his current wife with him and had demanded the best table in the house.

"Jess took one look at my face," Carla said, "and must've figured out that something was wrong."

Jess had taken Carla aside, and had gotten it out of her that this was her ex, the man who'd beaten her when they were married. Jess had told her to take off until the s.o.b. left.

Carla conveyed all this while dripping on my kitchen floor. I grabbed some kitchen towels out of a drawer, and she used them to dry her face and arms. But her clothes were still sopping wet.

"Come on." I led the way to the master bedroom, Noelle still propped on my hip.

Carla was slightly taller than me and thinner. "My stuff will be a little baggy on you but…" I selected a pair of black fleece pants and a long-sleeved, dark green tee shirt from my dresser drawers.

Leaving her alone to change, I placed Noelle again in the play yard in the study. She plopped down on her diaper-padded butt and began rummaging through her toys. I smiled down at her and stroked her thin cap of silky hair, a slightly lighter shade of reddish brown than my own.

Carla emerged a couple of minutes later, drier and more composed. "Sorry I burst in on you like that. I must've sounded like a lunatic."

"No apologies needed. You forget that I also have an ex-husband." Although all he'd done was bonk a cello player in the Baltimore Symphony, where he played the violin. He'd never hit me.

I tried to imagine how I would've reacted if he had. Considering how young and naive I was when I'd married him—honestly, I wasn't sure what I would've done.

"Hey," I said, "if you'll watch Noelle, I'll go down to the diner and see if he's still there."

She quickly nodded.

I pointed to the play yard. *What a misnomer.* How could a thirty-inch by forty-inch space with mesh walls be considered a *yard*? Noelle certainly didn't think much of it since she repeatedly escaped from it.

"Watch out. She knows how to get out of that thing." I paused, feeling a tad guilty. Carla had no clue what she was getting into. "And keep an eye on the puppy. He's not completely potty-trained yet."

Ignoring the guilt, I grabbed a sweater and an umbrella and got out of there.

As I hustled out the door, Buddy shoved past me. I didn't try to stop him, figuring he needed a break from the anxiety of watching over Noelle as much as I did.

I didn't have his leash but I knew he'd stick close. We jogged down Main Street and around the diner to the large gazebo Jess had added last summer, for outdoor dining. It was deserted on this chilly, damp evening.

We darted under its roof, and I told Buddy to lie down and stay. He sank to the wooden planks and placed his head on his paws. I'm pretty sure I heard him sigh.

My plan was to go through the kitchen and peek over the saloon-style swinging doors that separated it from the dining area. But that doorway was blocked by the broad, plaid-flannel-clad back of Johnny Redmond.

He was a bit heavyset, not fat but big all over, with a barrel chest. And he was our resident sheriff's deputy, although out of uniform at the moment.

I reached up and tapped his shoulder.

He started and turned his head. "Oh, hi," he said quietly. I could barely hear him over the male voice coming from the dining area.

Johnny shifted sideways so I could see over one door.

The dining area was decorated with green garlands around the edge of the ceiling, red ornaments hanging from them. At each end of the room were banners advertising the fancy New Year's Eve dinner Jess had planned, steak and lobster with all the trimmings for forty dollars a person.

I smiled as my mouth watered.

Then the sight of Carla's ex, Caleb Wilkes, wiped the smile away. He wasn't hard to spot. Six-foot, middle-aged, slightly overweight and wearing a toupee, he was expounding in a too-loud voice to his current wife about his past business successes.

I didn't know the whole story, but according to Carla, many of those so-called successes had been failures.

Sheez, Louise, can he be any more of a cliché? Ms. Snark commented internally.

Hmm, I hadn't heard from Ms. Snark that much recently. I'd been too busy juggling motherhood with helping Will run our new private investigations agency to pay much attention to the rest of the world. The world that the snarky side of myself, whom I'd dubbed Ms. Snark, loved to comment on.

Fortunately, she was less inclined lately to comment on *my* activities, which, in the past, she'd often found lacking in intelligence and finesse.

"Jess called me," Johnny whispered. "But I'm not sure what I should do. I mean, it's not against the law to be obnoxious."

"Maybe it should be," I whispered out of the side of my mouth, my eyes still on the couple seated at the large table normally reserved for parties of four or more.

A sound from Johnny that was somewhere between a snort and a snicker.

The wife was trying to get Wilkes to lower his voice. She was a couple of decades his junior, a foot shorter, and slightly overweight, but with distinct curves—*pleasingly plump*, my mother would call her. A halo of blonde kinky curls surrounded a smooth face with a peaches-and-cream complexion.

Between efforts to shush her husband, she polished the silverware with her napkin, then carefully straightened everything in front of her. Her side of the table looked like a photo in *Good Housekeeping* magazine.

Jess Randall and her new evening-shift waitress were hustling to keep the dishes flowing to the other tables. Jess kept flicking nervous glances at Carla's ex, who was making the other diners visibly uncomfortable.

"Yup, DeeDee," Wilkes exclaimed, "my establishment's gonna put this podunk town on the map."

His wife frowned at him. The slight crow's feet around her blue eyes had me adding a few years to my initial estimate of her age. Probably early thirties.

No wonder his businesses fail, Ms. Snark observed internally, *when he insults his potential customers like that.*

Jess is an introvert and basically easygoing, but she has her limits. Red-faced, she marched over to Carla's ex. "Mr. Wilkes, I'm going to have to ask you to leave."

Wilkes stood, trying to intimidate her with his height.

But petite Jess—in her usual uniform of jeans, tee shirt and apron, dark hair pulled back in a short ponytail—stood her ground. Fists on her hips, she glared up at him.

Johnny pushed the door open and stepped into the dining area. He crossed his arms over his broad chest and cleared his throat.

Wilkes looked our way and froze, the sneer on his face fading. He stomped out of the diner. His wife trailed behind, her cheeks flushed.

I felt a pang of sympathy for her. My first husband had been a bit boorish, although not as bad as Wilkes.

The tension level in the diner quickly lowered, and folks went back to relaxing over their meals.

Jess came over to us, and we all stepped back into the kitchen. Her gaze on the ceiling, she said, "Dear God in heaven, thank you!" I suspected that was a true prayer of thanksgiving, since I'd never heard her take the Lord's name in vain.

Scrubbing a hand over her face, she turned to Johnny. "And thank you."

He put his big hand on her shoulder, squeezed it, then let go.

I hid a smile. I was one of the few people who knew that they were engaged.

"Carla's pretty shook," I said.

Jess nodded. "I thought she was going to have a heart attack when they walked in."

"Why did he come *here* for dinner, of all places?" Johnny asked.

She stared at us for a beat. "Because he's rented one of Edna's new shops, to open a bakery. He's now my competition."

Color me confused…and distressed.

Jess barely kept the diner afloat as it was. But how was a bakery her competition?

She moved in closer to us. "He was bragging," she said, in a low, shaky voice, "that not only would he have pastries and fresh bagels in the mornings, but also savory ham and cheese scones at lunchtime."

Johnny put his arm around her shoulders.

I shook my head. "What kind of obnoxious jerk comes into a competitor's place of business and starts spewing such crapola?"

"An abusive jerk," Jess said, her face grim.

CHAPTER TWO

Back at my house, Carla seemed much calmer. She had blown dry her shoulder-length brown hair—now streaked with some gray—and was playing patty-cake with Noelle on the loveseat in the study. The puppy was curled up on top of her shoe, sound asleep.

When I told her that Jess had thrown her ex out of the diner, her eyebrows arched almost to her hairline.

"I hope you don't mind," she said. "I put my clothes in your dryer. They should be dry in another fifteen minutes or so. Why don't you take a break in your bedroom for a little while, and I'll keep Noelle entertained?"

She didn't have to ask me twice. I left a damp Buddy curled up on his bed and went down the hall to the master bedroom.

Peeling off wet socks, I replaced them with my warmest slippers and plopped down on the stuffed armchair by the slider that led to our back deck. I loved to sit here, stare at our long grassy backyard—bordered by palm trees, Southern pines and palmetto bushes—and contemplate life.

This was the closest I'd ever come to feeling "normal," whatever that is, and feeling content at the same time. Looking back, my whole life had been a struggle between seeking normalcy and rebelling against it.

It all started when my mother named me Marcia. Only she wouldn't let people pronounce it the more normal way—like Marsha. No, it was *Mar-see-a*.

Wait, no, it all started when my mother—the daughter of a Methodist minister, so she should've known better—married an Episcopal priest.

And, yes, they can marry! The joke I've always loved and my parents both hated was that the Episcopal Church was Catholic Light. All the rituals, half the guilt.

But not completely free of guilt...

So, there I was, a normal, energetic kid, saddled with an abnormal name, and a preacher's brat to boot. My mother had been ultra-strict with me and my brother, knowing that the "old biddies" (Mom's word, not mine) in my father's church would be quick to shame us if we got too rambunctious or dared to let a swear word slip out.

Fast-forward thirty-seven years—past my "normal" first marriage that lasted all of two years, and the "normal" divorce due to adultery, then the "normal" commitment phobia, overcome by the abnormal patience of my second husband—to the birth of our daughter.

Ah, but the struggle did not end there. What to name this child?

Ironically, I wanted to be normal and name her after our mothers.

But I encountered resistance from Will. And after three years of marriage, I finally found out why I'd never met his mother.

"She sided with my ex-wife," Will had finally admitted.

"Wha'?" My mouth had fallen open.

"She'd grown to love Davy as much as I had." He'd paused. "Maybe more than she loved me." When his first marriage had ended, he'd also lost the stepson he'd loved as his own…and apparently his mother as well.

But Will's reaction to the demise of his marriage had been very different from mine. I'd feared commitment and also the concept of offspring that would tie one to an ex for life. He'd desperately sought a new relationship so he could have children of his own, to fill the void left by the loss of little Davy.

But somehow we'd both overcome our fears and obsessions, and finally here we were, married and parents.

And we had ended up naming our daughter a normal name—Claire for my mother, and Noelle because she was born ten days before Christmas. Claire Noelle, but we would call her Noelle.

"An angelic name!" my mother had commented at the time of her birth.

Ha!

Fast forward a year to Noelle's first birthday celebration last week, and my mother was laughing hysterically. "What goes around, comes around." She'd grabbed Noelle just before she'd nabbed the string of lights on the lowest branch of our Christmas tree.

"I wasn't this bad," I'd protested.

My mother had arched an eyebrow in the air. "Yeah, you were."

A crash from the front of the house yanked me back to the here-and-now. Then my husband's voice, "Claire Noelle, what have you done?"

◆———◆

Fifteen minutes later, we'd accepted Carla's apology and had cleaned up the broken lamp. Carla grabbed up her now dry clothes and hustled out the door, while I was busy stopping Noelle from pulling yet another lamp off a table via its electric cord.

She giggled, apparently thinking this was an excellent new game. And I sighed, mentally scratching Carla off our potential babysitter list.

I fed the baby her dinner, Will read to her, and we bedded her down for the night. With any luck, she'd stay in her crib.

Then Will and I sat down at the dining table near the slider in the living room, our own dinner spread out in front of us— chicken and all the fixings that Will had brought home from KFC.

I was trying not to fall asleep in my mashed potatoes and gravy. It had been a long day.

"What all do we need to do before Ben and family arrive?" Will asked.

"Clean the training center and guest suite." Both of which were located in the part of our house that had once been my 1960s-vintage cottage. "And I want to move Sugar's crate into the study, so Ben's kids don't mess with her."

Sugar was a cream-colored Labrador I had trained for a female naval petty officer suffering from PTSD. I'd begin the human phase of the training after the first of the year.

"Maybe our bedroom would be better," Will said.

"Probably, if we can find room for it." I ate some potatoes. "What time are you leaving in the morning?"

Will shook his head, his mouth full of fried chicken.

"You're not leaving early? I thought you had to keep an eye on this guy until he messed up."

Will finished chewing and swallowed. "He already did. Mess up, that is. Shortly after I called you, he came out of his house in running clothes and took off down the street. I guess he figured it was dark enough, no one would see that he wasn't a 'seriously impaired accident victim.'" He made air quotes.

"I got a video of him running, from the back, but I needed his face. So I drove past him, stopped several blocks ahead, and recorded him as he ran under a streetlight. Got his face real clear in that one. I scrunched down on the front seat, so he wouldn't realize the truck was occupied when he ran past it."

Will wasn't giving me all those details just to brag. I was in training to be a licensed private investigator myself. And the bulk of our cases, so far, had been potential insurance fraud investigations like this one.

Will helped himself to a second piece of chicken, laid it on his plate. "I stayed down until I heard the slap of his sneakers as he circled back to his house, and then waited another couple of minutes to be sure he'd gone back inside."

"So the case is closed," I said, relieved that we had one less thing to deal with over the next few days.

"It will be, as soon as I send the videos off to the company." Will grinned. "His claim will be denied, and we'll get a nice, fat check....So, how was your day? Besides the usual chaos with Noelle and the puppy, that is."

I told him, leaving out that usual chaos and focusing on the events around Carla's ex showing up in town.

"Does Edna know this guy plans to compete with the diner?" Will asked. "I thought she wasn't going to allow that. Don't the leases contain a non-compete clause?"

"Hmm, I'd forgotten about that. I'll talk to her in the morning."

He nodded, then grinned at me again. "*After* you sleep in. I'm getting up with Noelle."

I smiled back. "Have I told you recently how much I love you?"

⊷——⊶

Edna Mayfair was not happy when I told her about the bakery planning to compete with Jess's diner for breakfast and lunch patrons.

In one of her bright muumuus, gray hair sticking out in all directions, she practically had steam coming out of her ears as she stomped down the motel's porch steps. She'd only recently switched to her winter footwear—moccasins rather than flip-flops—but they did little to improve her professional image, or lack thereof.

I'd tried to talk her into putting on her official hotelier outfit, black stretch pants and a purple blouse, but no dice. "Not wearing that get-up again unless I have to. The motel's Susanna's to run now." And then she'd taken off down the street.

Buddy and I hurried to catch up. Anyone who knew our octogenarian town matriarch also knew better than to cross her. But recalling Caleb Wilkes's attempt to intimidate Jess, I wasn't sure what would happen. I needed to go along as protector, although I wasn't sure which of them I'd end up protecting.

The exteriors of the buildings were painted in various pastel shades, reminding me of scoops of pink, mint green and lavender sherbet. The fourth shop in the row, a pale blue, already had a sign up above the door—*Wilkes Bakery*. Hammering sounded from within.

Edna didn't bother to knock. She threw open the door and marched in. Buddy and I followed on her heels.

The large room smelled of paint, with smears of various shades of light grey on one white-primered wall.

That was all I could take in before Edna stopped suddenly and I almost ran into her.

"You're not Caleb Wilkes," she said.

The man who was installing shelves along the side wall stopped his hammering and turned. He was tall and muscular, with light brown skin and a shaved head. "No, I'm not," he said in a neutral tone.

"Where is he?" Edna demanded.

The man made a face that was hard to interpret. "Not here."

"I can see that, young man. When will he be back? I need to talk to him about his lease."

"You can talk to me about it," the man said.

Edna gave him an imperious look and opened her mouth.

I stepped forward. "And you are?" I asked in a soothing tone.

"Leroy Jenkins, Wilkes's partner."

Edna's cheeks pinked, and not from anger this time. "I, uh… I'm sorry. I thought you were part of the construction crew."

The man stared at her for a beat, his expression unreadable. I suspected he was trying to decide if he should take offense at that assumption.

Then he flashed a small smile. "Understandable." He held up

his hammer. "I *was* constructing."

We all chuckled, the tension broken.

"So, what about the lease?" he asked.

"It has a non-compete clause in it," Edna said, "which y'all are breakin'."

He made that face again. I decided it was his I'm-not-happy face.

"I've yet to see the lease, even though my name was supposed to be on it too. How exactly are we competing with someone?"

Edna turned to me. "Tell him."

I described the scene at the diner yesterday, leaving out Wilkes's connection to Carla. And I tried to waltz around just how obnoxious his partner had been, but the man could probably read between the lines.

He sighed. "I wondered why he added bagels and savory scones to the menu. Neither are my specialties."

"Your specialties?" I said.

"Yeah. I'm the talent. I do the baking, Caleb provides the capital." He rubbed a hand over his shaved head. "Look, I'll talk to him. We'll take out those items from the menu that would compete with the diner."

"No, we won't!" A voice from behind us.

I whirled around. Buddy growled softly, the hair standing up along his spine.

Carla's ex, Caleb Wilkes, filled the doorway. "That clause refers specifically to the other 'shops on Main Street.'" He made air quotes. "No mention of the diner."

"Well, I meant the diner as well," Edna said from beside me. I could hear her teeth grinding. "We're trying to attract new businesses to the town, not put existing ones out of business."

"That's not what the lease says," Caleb said. "Our menu stands."

Edna stomped her foot. Again, it would've been more impressive with different footwear. "The lease *does* say that I can terminate it for any reason, with ninety-days notice. Consider this your notice. Be out of here in ninety days, or less."

A thud behind us as Leroy's hammer hit the floor. "What?" he shouted.

Wilkes took a menacing step forward. "We'll see about that. I'll sue you, and my lawyers will tie things up in court for years. You'll be dead long before the case is resolved."

I sucked in air. Edna gasped beside me.

And suddenly Leroy was between us and his partner. "Calm down, Caleb. I'm sure we can work all this out."

Wilkes tried to push past him, but Leroy grabbed his arms. He jerked his head toward the door, indicating we should get out of there.

Good idea! Ms. Snark said internally.

I took Edna by the elbow and hustled her out the door. It slammed behind us.

Out on the boardwalk, we could hear loud arguing from within the bakery. We didn't stick around to see who won.

⊷——⊶

The next few days went by in a whirlwind, and I forgot all about Carla's ex.

Christmas dinner was at Mom's and Clint's new place, an hour from us in the center of the state. Clint's children and stepchildren were also there, along with their families. It was quite a houseful.

We'd agreed to my brother and his family staying with us because, one, we had a guest suite, and two, my mother and my sister-in-law did not get along. But they were on their best behavior for Christmas, and the day went well, with lots of laughter and good food—Mom's a much better cook than I am.

Noelle was a hit with the cousins, especially my young niece who'd decided the baby was her own personal live doll.

I smiled, enjoying the afterglow as we drove home, my brother's rental car following us. We turned onto Main Street, went past the shops and the motel.

Wait! There were lights on in the diner, in the kitchen area. It was supposed to be closed for the holiday. Had Jess left them on for security? We didn't usually worry much about that in our relatively crime-free town.

"Can you let me and Buddy out here," I said to Will in a low voice, so as not to wake Noelle in the backseat of the truck's extended cab. "If Jess or Carla are in there, I'd like to check on them. And I'll give Buddy his evening walk while I'm at it."

"Sure." Will pulled over to the curb and let us out.

The diner's front door was locked. Buddy and I went around to the back. I turned the knob on the back door. Not locked.

The sight beyond it brought me up short.

Petite Jess stood on a stool, in apron and hairnet, next to the big metal worktable that dominated the center of the kitchen. She was pounding the crapola out of a large clump of dough.

"Hey," I called out, "what'd that dough ever do to you?"

Jess jumped and almost fell off her stool.

"Sorry, didn't mean to startle you." I took a step into the kitchen. "What are you so worked up about?" I'd only seen her pound dough like that once before, when she was mad at her now deceased first fiancé.

She turned toward me. Tear streaks marred her cheeks, but her eyes were hard and angry. She pointed to a crumpled ball of paper on the floor. "That man had the audacity to tape one of those to the outside of the diner's window."

Telling Buddy to stay by the door, I stepped over and picked up the paper. I smoothed it out against my leg, then let out a gasp when I read the words: *Come one, come all, to our Grand Opening Gala at Wilkes Bakery, New Year's Eve, noon to six. Free food and soft drinks.*

The same day as the diner's New Year's Eve dinner! That started at five-thirty, and certainly wasn't free. Few people would be likely to go to both.

"That man," Jess growled, punching the dough in front of her. "I'm gonna kill him!"

⬦————⬦

The next morning was filled with a flurry of packing and loading up my brother's rental car.

I hugged all the kids, including my eldest nephew, now a teenager. He acted like he didn't want me to, but once I'd gotten my arms around him, he hung on for a moment. "Love you too, kiddo," I whispered in his ear. He let go, blushing and ducking his head.

Ben gave me a long hug, then tweaked my nose. "Take care of yourself and your little family, Munchkin."

"You too," I said, a small lump in my throat. "Safe travels."

When they were gone, I lingered on the front porch. I hadn't realized how much I'd missed my brother and the kids. Perhaps motherhood was giving me a new appreciation for family.

I shook my head slightly to clear it. It was a beautiful day—high sixties, low humidity, and a slight breeze. I stepped back inside to ask Will if he would watch Noelle while I went for a ride on my mare.

"Go for it," he said. "I'll keep things together here."

I chuckled. "I'll settle for keeping everybody alive."

Forty-five minutes later, we'd finished a nice romp around the back fields, Buddy loping alongside. I pointed Niña back toward Main Street. I'd cool her down while checking out what progress had been made with the shops during the last few days, while I'd been preoccupied with family.

Most had signs up now. Besides the bakery, there were a clothing boutique, a shoe store, a gift shop, a kitchen and bath store, a wine shop, and a bookstore—I would definitely be checking that one out when it opened. And on the very end was a bike rental place.

What a great idea! Tourists could bike around town, or even to the lake a few miles away.

I shivered a little, recalling some not-so-pleasant events at that lake, near Valentine's Day two years ago.

Curious, I guided Niña around to the back of the buildings. Things weren't quite as neat there, with several piles of construction debris scattered about. But each back door now had a small stoop made of seasoned lumber, with one step up to it. Just high enough to keep water from getting in under the doors during an intense rainstorm, which we had plenty of in Florida.

Wary of nails, I steered Niña in a wide berth around the piles of debris, keeping a sharp eye on the ground.

Suddenly she snorted and stopped abruptly, pitching me

forward against her neck. Then she veered to the left, farther away from the nearest pile of scrap wood. I was almost unseated.

"Whoa, girl." I tightened the reins, something I rarely have to do. "Take it easy." I examined the ground around us, trying to figure out what had upset her.

Niña is what horse people call a push-button horse. Very well-mannered, she does exactly what I tell her to do. So something had to have upset her, but I couldn't figure out what.

I loosened the reins again, nudged her with my knees. She refused to move.

The breeze picked up some, and a faint coppery odor reached my nose, mixed with something a bit more pungent.

Buddy started toward the smell.

"Come back here, boy!"

That's what had Niña spooked. An animal had died in or near that pile, or maybe someone had thrown garbage amongst the construction debris.

I dismounted and pulled the reins over the mare's head to lead her away. But when I glanced back at the pile, I froze.

Something was sticking out of it that shouldn't be there. A man's leather work glove...and it wasn't flat.

My stomach did a somersault. I was pretty sure there was a hand inside that glove.

CHAPTER THREE

Heart hammering, I called Will, belatedly realizing I should've called 911.

"Hey sweetheart, what's up?"

"Uh, I found a body, I think… Behind the shops."

"A what?"

"A body, as in a corpse…or maybe he's not dead." I swallowed hard. "I don't, um, know for sure," I stammered. I was more than a little shaken.

Not that I hadn't seen dead bodies before, more than any person should ever have to see. But rarely had carnage come to Mayfair.

Yes, there'd been that near-drowning out at the lake, and Jess's fiancé had been killed on their farm, on the fourth of July a few years ago. And we'd had occasional miscreants come to town—stalkers, vandals, and an arsonist once.

But no one had actually been killed here, at least not in recent years.

I realized Will was talking, saying something about me coming home so he could come check things out.

"Okay. I've got Niña with me. I'll take her to the barn and come home."

I led Niña around the end of the buildings and across the street to the pasture gate. Since it was a mild day, she wasn't sweaty, and I could get away with not rubbing her down. I stopped just inside the gate, took off her saddle and bridle and slapped her rump. She jogged off.

I slung the saddle and bridle on top of the fence and turned toward my house. Will was trotting toward me.

"I got Sherry to babysit," he called out. When he got closer, he added, "Show me this body."

Back behind the buildings, Will leaned carefully over the debris pile and touched the part of the glove where a wrist would be, if there was a hand in it.

He gave me a dismayed look that said there was indeed a hand.

Will clasped the wrist more firmly. "No pulse."

My stomach flip-flopped and I felt lightheaded. I leaned a shoulder against the clapboard exterior of the shop and made myself take a deep breath.

Will used his phone to take photos from different angles, then moved a couple of scraps of wood. He reached his hand in and felt the person's neck. "No pulse there either."

I swallowed hard.

He stepped back, tapped on his phone, and held it to his ear.

Curiosity got the better of squeamishness. I took a step forward to peer into the hole he'd made in the pile.

The face staring back at me was that of Caleb Wilkes—Carla's ex.

⬥

Crapola! Joe Brown was assigned to the case.

I try to like most people, but Detective Joseph Brown tends to make that difficult. He is as dull as his name. With brown hair and eyes, his roly-poly body was always clad in poorly fitting brown suits. Today's was paired with a yellow shirt and striped tie.

He and Will had been partners briefly, so Will could "show him the ropes" after he'd transferred into our county from another jurisdiction. Will had never said anything negative about the man, but he'd seemed relieved when he was allowed to go back to working solo.

My experiences with Detective Brown had convinced me that he took the easiest route to solving a case, without really looking at all possibilities.

"I understand a lot of people in town weren't happy with this guy," Brown said to me now.

Johnny Redmond, in his deputy's uniform, was watching the detective out of the corner of his eye, as he helped another deputy search the ground behind the shops for evidence.

"Any particular person who's got it in for Mr. Wilkes?" Brown asked.

I hesitated, then shook my head. Not any *one* particular person. There were *several* people who would fit that description.

"Who?" Brown demanded. Apparently, he'd caught my hesitation.

"He's…he was a pretty obnoxious person."

"I hear his ex-wife lives near here," he said. "No love lost there, I would assume."

"They've been divorced for years," I said, probably too quickly. "Carla wouldn't risk the good life she has now, just to take revenge for past slights." Being abused is a lot worse than a "slight," but I was minimizing for a good cause.

"She's always said," I crossed my fingers behind my back, "'living well is the best revenge.'" She'd never said that, to my knowledge, thus the crossed fingers to negate the fib.

What she had said was that she didn't care what her ex did as long as he left her alone. That was a few years ago, in response to the news that Caleb had remarried—to the wife before this latest one.

"His new wife," I said, "what's she going to inherit?"

"I'll ask the questions, Ms. Banks-Haines, thank you very much. I hear Ms. Cummings manages the diner, which would make this new bakery of Mr. Wilkes's a competitor."

"She's the dinner-shift manager, not the owner. He wouldn't have been competing with her." Okay, that's a hair split, but…

"Harumph," Brown said and walked away.

Johnny shot him a worried look. And he had good reason to be worried.

As bad as it was that the detective was sniffing around Carla as a prime suspect, it would be worse when he found out how much Wilkes was hated by Carla's boss—and Johnny's fiancée—Jess Randall.

While Will was being questioned by his former partner, I went home to rescue our neighbor from Noelle's exhausting presence. The child was a perpetual motion machine.

But I found her sitting contentedly on Sherie's lap on the sofa, while the older woman read her the story of *The Three Little Pigs*.

Sherie scrunched her brown face up into a mean expression as she read the wolf's lines. When she got to the "huff and puff and blow your house down" part, she and Noelle blew out air at the same time. Although in Noelle's case it was more of a juicy raspberry.

I sat down across the living room from them and observed, as Sherie finished the story.

Her hair, in a neat chignon on the back of her head, was now mostly gray, with thin streaks of black left. But there were still only a few wrinkles on her face, despite the fact that she would be sixty-nine on her next birthday.

Susanna Mayfair, Sherie's contemporary, was the same— crow's feet around her eyes, and one furrow along her forehead that was accentuated when she frowned, but her cheeks were smooth. They'd both grown up in Mayfair so I couldn't help but wonder if there was some kind of youth elixir in the water.

Or at least I could hope that there was.

The puppy waddled into the room, whining. We'd moved his piddle pad from the kitchen to next to the slider in the living room, hoping to transition him to going outside soon. But he seemed to be confused by the change.

I stood, scooped him up and plopped him on the pad. He gratefully lifted his leg and peed. I could almost hear him sighing.

If only human beings' lives were that simple.

"The end," Sherie said, and she and Noelle both clapped, the child chortling. Sherie put her down on the floor.

Within seconds, the puppy was running around in circles, with Noelle crawling after him and giggling hysterically.

Trying to ignore their frenetic energy, I focused on Sherie, who was asking me what was going on. I gave her a succinct summary of finding the body, and of the sheriff's department's activities.

Somewhere in there, Sherie's hand had flown to her mouth. Now she was shaking her head. "I love Edna dearly, but sometimes her attempts to improve the town tend to backfire."

I snorted. "That's putting it mildly. More like they blow up in our faces."

So far, Edna's plan to build an ice-skating rink to attract winter tourists had led to the discovery of a thirty-year-old corpse, and the skating rink had never happened. Then her Halloween haunted house had ended up a lot scarier and more dangerous than she'd intended, and her Independence Day Extravaganza had concluded with Jess's first fiancé's death.

And as the chair of the local Chamber of Commerce, Sherie often ended up picking up the pieces after these disasters.

Hopefully, this murder didn't cause the other shop owners to want out of their leases. Yes, Edna had family money, but surely the fortune her late brother had accumulated had its limits.

⊷──⊶

I was having an argument with myself. The detective in me, and the friend, desperately wanted to know more about Caleb Wilkes—his business dealings, who his enemies might be. Surely, there were plenty of people who hated him even more than Carla and Jess did.

But my practical side was objecting to ordering a background check on him. Our fledgling PI agency could ill afford an expense that wouldn't be reimbursed by a paying client.

The internal debate was still raging when Will came home.

"Anything new?" I asked.

He shook his head. "It's early on yet." He swooped down and picked up the baby as she was about to grab the puppy's tail.

"Hey," I said, "now that you're no longer with the sheriff's department, are you willing to tell me honestly what you think of Joe Brown?"

Will shrugged. "He's a little drab as a person, but he's a competent detective."

"You're not just saying that?"

"No, he's…well, he's what I think of as a plodder. He plods along, putting together the evidence, but he usually solves his cases, eventually."

"Mm-hm, and do you think he gets the right culprit?"

Will had settled on the sofa, across the room from me, with Noelle on his knee. He glanced my way, then broke eye contact, focused intently on the baby's face as he bounced her gently up and down. She gurgled with pleasure.

"Most of the time he gets it right," he finally said.

"Mm-hm." We both knew of at least one time when he'd gotten it spectacularly wrong.

"My impression," I said, "is that he jumps to conclusions too quickly."

Will shrugged again. "You have to develop a theory of the case, what you think happened, in order to have a place to begin."

"You don't think he tries to make the evidence fit his theory?"

He paused so long, still focused on the baby, that I thought he wasn't going to answer me. Finally, he said, "A seasoned detective has good instincts, and they're usually right."

"In other words, the first theory of the case they develop is usually what really happened?"

He nodded, looking relieved.

Not so quick there, buddy-boy, Ms. Snark commented internally.

"How often was your first theory correct?" I said out loud.

"About ninety percent of the time."

"Uh-huh, and how often has Brown's theory been correct?"

Will froze for a second, then sighed. "About eighty percent of the time."

I started shaking my head. He opened his mouth, but I cut him off. "Eighty percent is not good enough when our friends are involved. They could all too easily end up in the twenty-percent-he-gets-wrong category."

"Mar-see-a," Will said slowly and emphatically, "we are *not* going to interfere in an active sheriff's department investigation."

"I wouldn't dream of it, but I'd like to order a background check on Wilkes." Our discussion had given me my answer to the internal debate.

I'd been tempted to just do it and not tell Will. But keeping secrets from him in the past had backfired, rather badly a couple of times.

"I would like to know," I continued, "who his other enemies may be. As obnoxious as he was, he's bound to have plenty."

Will's expression was thoughtful. After a moment, he said, "We won't do anything with the information until an arrest is made. If we think Joe's got it wrong, we'll ask whoever he's arrested to hire us, for a dollar."

I grinned. "At which point, our investigating becomes totally legit."

Will nodded, returning the grin. "Yup, the defendant has the right to hire their own investigator."

◆———◆

Once I'd emailed Elise Roberts—our background-check person and only employee—with Wilkes's name and as much information as I had on him, I asked Will if he could watch Noelle for a bit. I wanted to go over to the diner and check on Jess. He thought that was a good idea.

I was startled to find the sign on the diner's door flipped over to *Closed*. A sense of foreboding accompanied me around to the back door. It was not locked.

I pulled it open and stepped inside, Buddy on my heels.

Jess sat on a stool at one corner of the large metal prep table, forehead resting on her arms crossed on the table. At the sound of the kitchen door clicking closed, she looked up. Her eyes were red and puffy.

"Surely you're not crying over Caleb Wilkes's death," I blurted out.

She pulled in air. "Not exactly." Then she shook her head. "I guess all this is reminding me of when Dan died."

My expression must have shown my confusion. She tilted her chin toward the doorway into the dining area.

I turned my gaze in that direction. Two deputies and Detective Brown were searching the tables, even pulling up the seats of the benches in the booths.

Poor Jess. Of course, this was bringing back bad memories.

She had been a suspect for a while in Dan's death, had even been arrested.

I hustled over to her and wrapped an arm around her shoulders. Her petite frame shuddered as she sank into the hug.

"What's going on here?" Joe Brown's voice from the dining area doorway.

At the same moment, the back door of the kitchen flew open.

"Arrest her!" Mrs. Wilkes screamed, standing in the doorway and pointing at Jess. "She killed my husband." Then she turned, sobbing, and ran back out the door.

CHAPTER FOUR

After the drama at the diner, I was ready to go home and try to unwind some from a stressful morning. But when I opened my front door, I found my husband standing in the middle of the living room, a stunned look on his face.

My chest tightened. "What?"

Shaking his head, he didn't answer.

My heart jumped into my throat. "What's happened? The baby?" I screeched.

"No, no, she's fine. She's napping." He took a deep breath. "But I just got the strangest phone call. Some guy claims I hit him last week, on Williston Road."

"Hit him?" I echoed, while trying to get my galloping heart under control. "Like, in a car crash?"

"Yeah, no, not another car. He said he was walking along the side of the road."

I shook my head. My brain was having trouble processing all this.

"It was the evening I was doing surveillance over that way," Will said. "The guy kinda laughed and said something like, maybe I didn't notice the bump…But I've run over someone before."

"What?" I yelped.

"It was when I was a rookie cop." He sank onto the sofa.

Patting my chest to calm my still thumping heart, I sat down beside him.

"We responded to a burglary in progress," he said. "The guy ran out of the house, right as we got there. I took off after him in the car, while my partner checked on the homeowners. The guy tripped and fell. I slammed on the brakes but was still doing about thirty when I ran over his leg. He had a pretty bad break, but he eventually recovered."

Will stopped, took another deep breath. "The thing is, that jarred the car quite a bit. It was like hitting a speed bump without slowing down. I know darn well I would've noticed if I hit someone who was standing up, or even if they were already lying in the road."

He shook his head again. "The guy said he didn't tell the police who hit him, and he was hinting that I should pay him off to keep silent."

My mouth fell open. "Crapola! He's blackmailing you?"

"Trying to. I called my old captain at the sheriff's department. He ran the guy's phone number. No record of it."

"So it's a disposable," I said. "Are you thinking this is a scam?"

"It's gotta be, because I know I didn't hit anyone that night. He said he has a picture of the back of my truck, by the way."

"Yeah, right. This guy gets hit by a truck and yet he's able to quickly pull out his phone and snap a photo as you're driving away?" I scoffed. "I don't think so. Did he say how much he wanted?"

"Not precisely. He said a few thousand would 'defray his medical expenses.'" Will made air quotes. "He claims he was in the hospital from then until today."

"There's no way this could be legit. Why wouldn't he go after our insurance if he was hurt that bad?"

"Exactly. But some people would get nervous, wonder if maybe they did hit him, and would pay to keep from being arrested."

"Arrested for what?"

"Hit and run. It's a serious charge."

I realized my mouth was hanging open again. I closed it.

"So, how are Jess and Carla holding up?" Will asked, apparently ready to change the subject.

"I didn't see Carla, but…" I filled him in on the police search of the diner and Mrs. Wilkes showing up to accuse Jess of murder.

"Did Joe take her seriously?" Will asked.

"Not sure. She ran off before anyone could say anything to her."

"I doubt her accusation will influence him. He'll collect the evidence and go by that."

"I hope you're right." I sighed, my insides heavy. "But why would she jump to the conclusion that Jess killed her husband?"

He shrugged. "She's probably just upset, and maybe saw that the deputies were searching the diner. People can get pretty irrational when a loved one is murdered."

Rustling noises, coming from the baby monitor on the breakfast bar, announced that Noelle was awake, and no doubt working on how to climb out of her crib.

By that evening, we'd heard nothing more about the murder investigation. As we were clearing the dinner dishes away, Will again suggested I sleep in the next morning, and then take a long ride.

I pointed out that I couldn't sleep in, as tomorrow was my day to feed the horses and muck stalls at the stable—Susanna and I shared those chores. "You're not working at all this week?" I asked.

He shook his head. "I put an outgoing message on the business line that the agency is on hiatus and invited people to leave a message, said we'd get back to them after New Year's."

"But we can't afford to lose any business."

"I doubt we will." He sighed. "Look, for my whole career, I've had my holidays interrupted by other people's grief. This time of year can be stressful for a lot of folks. There are more bar fights, more car accidents, more domestic violence calls. This year, I'm going to celebrate that I don't have to deal with all that anymore."

"You've earned it," I said. "But I can't help worrying about the money."

Will shrugged. "We're doing okay, and you'll be getting your training fee for Sugar soon."

"But what if that guy sues us?"

"What guy?"

"The one who said you hit him."

Will turned from the sink and gently took me by the shoulders. "Sweetheart, I did *not* hit anyone. The guy's a con man. When I called my captain earlier, he said he would check with the other departments in the area for similar cons. My guess is the guy has done this before."

I nodded, but the whole mess was making me nervous. My husband might be blamed for a hit-and-run he didn't do, and my friends might be charged for a murder they didn't commit.

I slept fitfully that night. At six a.m., I gave up and slipped carefully out of bed so as not to disturb Will. I went into my daughter's room and sat in the rocker in the corner, watching her sleep.

The room smelled of baby powder, and Noelle's face was so sweet.

Ha, Ms. Snark said internally, *only because she's asleep.*

I didn't argue, but truth be told, I was glad my child was the way she was. She went after what she wanted and wasn't afraid of obstacles. It was an attitude that would serve her well in adulthood.

But first, we had to get her *to* adulthood in one piece.

She opened one eye and met my gaze. After a beat, she grinned. "Ma-ma."

A warm, gooey feeling filled my chest. I stood and picked her up, cuddled her against me. "Well, don't you have an extensive vocabulary now—*dada*, *doggy*, *Neeyee* for Niña, and now *mama*."

She reached up and patted my cheek. "Ma-ma."

I did take advantage of Will being home.

After the stalls were mucked and the other horses were fed, Niña, Buddy and I went for a long ride. But we couldn't run as much as we once had, because of Buddy's age—I didn't want to give my old boy a heart attack.

We avoided the shops' area and found no fresh corpses, unless you count the roadkill on Highway 25. Looked like it might've been a squirrel, poor thing.

We crossed the country road, unduly glorified with the name "highway," and moved into the woods. Even in winter, there was more shade than sunshine. Palm trees and pines don't lose their leaves or needles completely. And even the live oaks, which are technically deciduous, replace their leaves as fast as they shed them.

Still it was a warmish day, hovering in the low seventies, so the temperature in the woods was comfortable with my light jacket.

Finally, we returned to the barn, feeling peaceful and pleasantly tired. I rubbed Niña down, brushed her coat to a dark sheen, and turned her loose. Of course, she immediately rolled in the dirt to scratch her back, undoing the good brushing I'd just given her.

Shaking my head but with a smile on my face, I turned toward home.

A blood-curdling scream erupted from the shops' area.

Heart slamming into overdrive, I took off running. Buddy struggled to keep up.

Mrs. Wilkes was standing in the open doorway of the bakery, looking inside and screaming bloody murder.

"What?" I yelled. "What happened?" *Please Lord, not another corpse.*

The woman stopped screaming but still stood frozen in the doorway.

I nudged her aside, took a step past her, and gasped.

One freshly painted, pale gray wall was covered with marks and symbols, in harsh shades of red, orange and green.

And below the graffiti were the words, *GO BACK TO WHERE YOU CAME FROM, OR ELSE.*

CHAPTER FIVE

I sucked in air. My stomach churned as I flashed back to a few Halloweens ago, when a vandal had haunted Mayfair, making our lives miserable.

I shook my head to clear it. Was the message from some bigot in town, aimed at Leroy Jenkins?

A niggly thought hovered in the back of my brain, out of reach.

The widow raised a trembling hand toward the mess, then pulled it back and clutched her hands together, as if afraid of getting paint on herself—even though we were across the room from the disfigured wall. "Could one of your friends…?" She trailed off, her voice shaky.

I jerked around toward her. "They wouldn't do something like this, Mrs. Wilkes."

"Delores, please, or Dee." Her cheeks were tear-streaked, but she attempted a feeble smile. "I'm sorry I screamed. I guess I'm a bit on edge right now."

"Understandably so."

"I owe your friend Jess an apology as well. I don't know what got into me, accusing her like that."

"I'm sure she'll understand." The niggling feeling grew stronger.

The purr of a powerful engine. Johnny's cruiser pulled up in front of the shop. A second later, he filled the doorway. "Edna reported screaming."

We stepped aside, and Johnny audibly sucked in air.

But he quickly took control. "Marcia, did you find this?"

"No, I came running when Mrs. Wil...uh, Dee started screaming."

"Okay, go intercept Edna for me, please."

I nodded. As I turned away, Johnny took out his phone and began taking photos of the garish display on the wall.

Edna was trotting past the first shop in the row, huffing a little.

I held out my hands in a wait gesture as Buddy and I jogged to meet her. "Johnny's got it under control. And nobody's hurt."

She stopped, catching her breath. "What happened?"

I told her about the graffiti and the threatening message. "Do you think it could be aimed at Leroy?" I asked. In other words, racially motivated.

For a Southern small town, we had very little bigotry. Edna and her brother had both set a good example from the get-go. The "old man," as long-term residents affectionately called him, was reputed to have rolled up his sleeves quite often to work beside his men—clearing fields and building the small arena that had housed the Mayfair Alligator Farm, long since defunct.

Susanna Mayfair and Sherie Wells had played together as

children. And Sherie and Edna were now best friends. They ran the town together, Edna as the unofficial mayor and Sherie as the chair of the Chamber of Commerce.

"If it is," Edna was saying, her voice firm, "I'm gonna do my best to find out who did it and run them outta town." She paused. "'Course, I can't imagine no one who's lived here for years would do somethin' like that."

It was the nature of small-town residents to blame newcomers for bad things that happened, but in this case, I had to agree with her.

Buddy sat at my side, panting heavily. "Look, I better get him home. Let me know if I can do anything to help."

Edna nodded. "I'm gonna tell Leroy that I'll pay to have the bakery repainted."

Recalling the garish colors, I shook my head slightly. It would take a lot of primer to cover up that mess.

A flash of bright blue in my peripheral vision. I turned toward a large green dumpster, beside the end shop. It hadn't been there yesterday.

Edna gestured toward it. "Just had that delivered. The construction crew's gonna clean up the mess in the back, soon as the sheriff's department gives the go ahead."

"Good." I squinted at the blue something hanging over the top edge of the open dumpster. Standing on tiptoe, I examined it more closely. It appeared to be a thin piece of rubber.

I reached up and nabbed it, then stared at the object dangling from my fingers.

A blue latex glove, with multicolored streaks of paint on it.

Back at the house, Will surprised me with a celebratory brunch. He'd put Noelle down for an early nap and made bacon, eggs and pancakes.

"Checked our business account," he said. "The payment from the insurance company was credited this morning."

I smiled. "So that's what we're celebrating."

"Yup, and they offered a bonus if we can get more evidence to cement their fraud case. I've got Elise digging deeper into that guy's background."

He pulled out a plate of pancakes that had been warming in the oven. "*And*, speaking of fraud, I got a call from my former boss. Our sheriff asked the sheriff of Levy County to do some checking around. He had his deputies canvas the residents along that stretch of Williston Road. Nobody saw or heard anything that evening that would indicate someone was hit, or that there was any kind of accident. Both sheriffs are convinced it's all a hoax."

"Phew." While I went to the kitchen sink and scrubbed my hands, I told him about the graffiti, my conversation with Dee Wilkes, and finding the latex glove.

"Johnny put it in an evidence bag and said they'd search the rest of the dumpster. Can they lift prints from the inside of a glove?"

"Probably. As long as they didn't get smudged as the glove was removed."

I opted to shove aside all thoughts of crime as we sat at the breakfast bar and enjoyed our meal.

We were clearing away the dishes when the doorbell rang. I ran to it, to keep whoever it was from pushing the button again. I didn't want Noelle waking up any sooner than necessary.

I pulled open the door and my mouth fell open.

Elise Roberts stood on our front porch—another "pleasingly plump" woman, fortyish, with dyed red hair. Her dog Rusty, a medium-sized mutt, also red-haired but in his case natural, stood next to her.

"Surprise!" She grinned at me, some papers in her hand. "My internet is down, so I figured I'd bring my report over in person."

"But you're out...I mean...you're not..." I broke off, unable to think of a polite way to ask what happened to her agoraphobia. For years, she hadn't left her house.

"May I come in?"

"Oh, of course. Sorry." I stepped back so they could enter. "Want some tea or coffee?" I remembered she avoided caffeine. "Um, I think I have decaf of both."

"Decaf tea would be great."

I gestured toward the breakfast bar. Elise hopped up on a stool, and Rusty laid down beside it.

They both looked good. I'd trained Rusty, while I was pregnant, to act as a comfort dog for Elise—to alert her when a panic attack was coming on and help soothe the anxiety. Apparently, he was helping more than I'd hoped for.

"So, you can go out and about now?" I said, as I put the tea kettle on.

Elise nodded. "I'm still careful where I go, no place crowded. And I make sure I can get out quickly if an attack starts."

"That's terrific." I knew that she had bought a car, through one of those online vendors, and being able to drive again had simplified her life. She could pick up her groceries curbside and make use of drive-thrus at the bank and pharmacy and such. But this was a whole new level.

Will came around the corner, Noelle in his arms.

Elise jumped a little and Rusty hopped to his feet, ready for duty. But she patted her chest and took a deep breath. "Sorry. You startled me. You must be Will."

He shifted the baby to one hip and came over, offering his hand. "And you must be Elise. Marcia told me you and your dog were matching redheads. Good to finally meet you in person."

Elise shook his hand. "Same here."

Noelle had hidden her face in her father's shoulder. Now she peeked out with one eye and babbled a few syllables.

I imagined her saying, *Who the heck are you?*

"Noelle," I said, "this is Elise. Elise, Noelle."

Elise took the baby's small hand and gave it a gentle shake. "Nice to meet you, Noelle."

She hid her face again, but then looked out and chortled.

Elise covered her face with her hands and played peekaboo with her. More chortling.

The kettle whistled. I brought mugs, tea bags and sugar to the breakfast bar and poured hot water.

Elise had won Noelle over. She even allowed Elise to hold her on her lap while Will and I perused the report on Caleb Wilkes.

"This guy's a piece of work," Elise commented. "Four failed businesses and three marriages and he's not quite fifty yet. Second marriage only lasted three years. Current one is five months old."

So he and Dee had been newlyweds. My heart ached for the woman. I hadn't liked the guy, but she had seen something good in him, had loved him, as had Carla at one time.

"Second wife is remarried," Elise said. "You want me to dig any deeper on her, or on anyone who might've been harmed when his businesses went under?"

"Not just yet," Will said, still reading over my shoulder.

The third page of the report listed criminal activity. Frequent domestic violence calls had come in during his first two marriages. But none in the current one.

My eye snagged on a note at the bottom of the page. Three restraining orders had been filed while he was married to Carla, two by her and the last one by him.

And the niggling feeling I'd been having off and on was back. *Carla!*

Could she have painted the graffiti on the bakery wall? It would've been aimed at Dee, not Leroy. I could imagine Carla *possibly* doing that, not wanting the woman around as a constant reminder of her ex.

But was she capable of killing him?

I shook my head, even as an image popped up in my mind's eye—of Carla, hands on hips, saying that she didn't care what her ex did as long as he left her alone.

Coming to her town and threatening her livelihood did not exactly fall under leaving her alone.

⇤——⇥

Elise lingered for a while, chatting. On the one hand, I was thrilled that she was able to visit with us in person, but I was also getting restless, anxious to talk to Carla.

"So," Elise asked, "what are you two doing for New Year's Eve?"

"The diner here is having a big fancy dinner," Will said, "with a DJ and dancing afterwards."

"My folks are coming over," I added. "They're going to the

early seating for dinner, then babysitting while we go over."

Elise cocked her head to one side. "I could babysit if you like, so you could all go together."

"Would you?" Will and I said in unison, our voices perhaps a little too eager.

"Does anybody around here set off fireworks on New Year's?" she asked.

"They're not allowed in town," Will said. "They spook the horses at the stable." He grinned. "And nobody's set any off since *I* moved here."

I chuckled. "Helps to have a resident lawman."

She matched our grins. "Then I'm good. What time?"

"Seven," I said. "The later seating is at seven-thirty."

We chatted a bit more, Noelle contentedly sitting on Elise's lap.

Why is she good for everyone but me?

Finally, Elise said her goodbyes. After she left, I told Will I wanted to check on Jess and Carla. He nodded and took the baby from me.

Leaving Buddy at home, I went to the diner, my true objective to have a chat with Carla. She would be coming on duty, and there was usually a lull this time of day, between the lunch and dinner crowds.

She wasn't there yet, but Leroy was, standing by the door into the kitchen and talking to Jess. "Don't worry, we're taking bagels and savory scones off our menu," he was saying as I approached them.

"What about your grand opening?" Jess asked.

"We're moving that to New Year's Day. That's when most of the other shops are opening as well."

Jess and I blew out air together.

"Thank you." Jess smiled, holding out her hand.

Leroy shook it. "I only want to get along with people here. We don't need to be competitors."

"I feel the same way," Jess said. "I may even buy some baked goods from you, for resale here at the diner. It's getting harder to keep up with demand."

"So," a male voice from behind us, "looks like you got what you were after."

We all whirled around.

Detective Joe Brown stood there, hands in the pockets of his brown trousers. He rocked back on his heels, a smile on his lips that didn't reach his eyes. "You got exactly what you wanted, Ms. Randall. No more competition."

Jess opened her mouth, but he cut her off.

"Turn around. You're under arrest." He made a come-here gesture to someone behind him.

Sheepishly, Johnny Redmond, in uniform, stepped forward. I hadn't noticed him hovering behind Brown.

"Cuff her," Brown said.

Johnny looked like he wanted to cry as he did so.

"Why are you arresting me?" Jess asked, her voice panicky.

"Because we had motive and now we have means. A board with blood on it was found buried in the compost pile at your farm. I'm betting it's gonna turn out to be Wilkes's blood."

My heart plummeted into my stomach. Carla also lived on Jess's farm.

I opened my mouth, but I couldn't make myself do it. I couldn't throw one friend under the bus to save another.

CHAPTER SIX

I managed to get about thirty seconds to talk to Jess before they hauled her away. Johnny was standing next to her, apologizing in a whisper, when I jumped in.

"You need to hire our agency," I said. "The fee will be one dollar a day."

She shook her head. "I couldn't–"

I interrupted. "Just do it, Jess!" My tone was much harsher than I'd normally use with a friend, especially one in trouble and upset. But Joe Brown was headed our way, a thunderstorm brewing on his face.

"Okay, you're hired," Jess said.

I stepped back, right as Brown got to us. "What the devil do you think you're doing?"

"Commiserating with a friend. Keep your chin up, Jess." I backed away from them, then turned and jogged home.

"Jess was just arrested, and she hired us," I said before I was even all the way in the front door.

"Good," Will replied. "I mean bad about the arrest, but good that she hired us."

I rushed into the study, sat down at my laptop and sent an email to Elise, ordering a background check on Jess. We'd learned the hard way to check out the clients, as well as the people we assumed were the bad guys. That way, there were no surprises, and sometimes a connection was discovered that was helpful.

I also gave Elise all the information I had, which wasn't much, on Delores Wilkes and Leroy Jenkins.

Reluctantly, I added a request for a background check on Carla, telling myself I was only being thorough.

"She's not the bad guy here," I muttered.

Or gal, in this case, Ms. Snark added in my head, but without her usual snarky tone.

I hesitated again, thinking about the money we'd be shelling out for these reports, but I typed *Rush* at the bottom of the email—which cost extra—and hit send.

Out in the living room, Will was sitting on our leather sofa, bouncing Noelle on his knee. His expression was grim, forehead furrowed, mouth a thin, straight line.

Noelle was imitating his expression.

The sight of her frown made me chuckle and eased the vise around my chest some. I managed to take a deep breath as I sat down next to Will.

I opened my mouth to say something…and burst into tears instead.

Will took a firmer grip on Noelle's arm with one hand and wrapped his other arm around my shoulders.

My tears subsided, and I swiped at my cheeks with the back of one hand.

"Feel better?" he asked.

"Not really."

He squeezed my shoulders. "We'll sort it out. It'll be okay."

⟢────⟣

Mid-morning the next day, I took Sugar and Buddy for a walk while Noelle napped and Will relaxed.

I ran into Edna doing the same with her two Springer Spaniels, Bennie and Bo. They were now eight, middle-aged in dog years, and they had settled down some. But not completely. When they saw Buddy, they started jumping around in excitement, getting their leashes twisted together.

Edna gave up on controlling them—which she did often, the main reason they weren't very well behaved. But they were loveable, as was Edna, so I kept my mouth shut about her lack of dog-training skills.

She let go of their leashes and I did the same with Buddy. The three dogs chased each other in circles in the motel parking lot. Sugar whined softly beside me, but she held the cover position.

I smiled down at her. The cover task is one of the most important ones I teach my dogs. Whenever their human stops moving, the dog faces behind them, literally watching their back and signaling with a tail thump and ear twitch if someone is approaching. It allows hypervigilant, anxiety-ridden veterans to be more relaxed out in public.

"Cover," I said, by way of encouragement. "Good girl!" I wouldn't offer a treat until we began moving again, as it would distract her now.

I expected Edna to stop to gossip, one of her favorite activities. But today she seemed like a woman on a mission.

"I was comin' to see you and Will," she said, without even bothering with introductory pleasantries. A social no-no in the South.

"What about?"

"I heard y'all are investigatin' that man's death, tryin' to clear Jess. I wanna pay for the investigation."

I opened my mouth to protest, secretly hoping she'd insist.

But she waved a hand in the air before I could say anything. "Y'all are just gettin' your agency off the ground. Ya can't afford expenses that ain't reimbursed. And it'll maybe take ya away from other jobs."

I shook my head. "We're on Christmas hiatus right now, but covering the expenses would be a godsend."

"Good, then it's settled. What have you found out so far?"

"Not much yet. We've ordered background checks on all relevant parties."

She nodded. "Good start. Y'all let me know if I can help." She began to turn away.

"Anything you know about the other tenants' backgrounds would help, or Wilkes's."

"Trust me, if I'd known as much about him as I know now, I wouldn't have rented to him. I hate to speak ill of the dead…"

I waited for the *bless his heart* that Southerners usually add to that sentence. It didn't come.

"…but I'm glad," she continued, "that obnoxious man ain't gonna be a part of our community anymore."

"Honestly, so am I."

Edna suggested I sit on the motel's Victorian-style front porch while she went to get the paperwork on the tenants. I settled on the over-wide porch swing, with my dogs at my feet, and she took "her boys" inside with her.

She came back in a couple of minutes without them, but with a thick file folder.

She might wear eccentric clothing—today's muumuu was neon green with orange flowers that made my eyes hurt—and she was pushing ninety, but she was still a shrewd businesswoman. She had run basic background checks on all the lease signers, but not other parties involved with their shops, so she had nothing on Leroy or Dee.

"I skimmed over the names of Wilkes's ex-wives," Edna said, "never realized he was Carla's ex, or I would've sent him packin'. And nothin' came back regarding a criminal record for him, not even domestic violence, even though I know…" She trailed off, perhaps not sure if I knew Carla's history.

"I know why he's her ex," I said. "And in a basic report, they probably wouldn't list times that he was charged and his wives later dropped the charges. They might only list convictions."

"That'll teach me." Edna shook her head. "Next time, I'll dig deeper."

"Let our background check person run the names of future tenants. She's a whiz. Definitely gets below the surface. And her rates are reasonable." Referring Edna to Elise made me feel better about both Edna paying our expenses and Elise babysitting on New Year's Eve.

Not much else came out of reviewing Edna's file. Only one tenant, the bike rental shop's owner, had a criminal history, for both using and distributing marijuana back in the '80s. "He's… what do they call it?" Edna said.

"An aging hippie?"

"Yeah, that's it."

With a small jolt, I realized Edna would've already been an adult when the cultural revolution of the 1960s was instigated, in part, by the hippies of that era. Yet many of her attitudes were quite modern, such as her abhorrence of racism.

"You want copies of these?" Edna asked. "My printer's got a copyin' function."

She is definitely a modern woman, Ms. Snark said inside, with a chuckle.

I hid a smile. "That would be great. I'll finish our walk and swing back around for the copies."

She jumped up and bustled inside.

The dogs and I strolled down the boardwalk in front of the new shops. All had their doors closed as it was a chilly day, only in the low sixties. I stopped at the end and admired the rows of bikes chained together beside the bike rental place.

I was pretty sure the aging hippie owner had overestimated the number of tourists we were likely to get in our little off-the-beaten-track town.

As I turned to head back the way we'd come, my nose picked up an unusual scent. It took me a moment to recognize it—marijuana smoke. I hadn't smelled it in years, not since I'd interviewed a graduate student at the University of Florida, trying to clear a young man of a murder charge. The grad student's small house in Gainesville had reeked of it.

I shrugged. Personally, I couldn't care less what the man did inside his closed shop, but I stopped in my tracks as another thought hit me.

What if Caleb Wilkes had caught this guy indulging? Would

he have threatened to turn him in?

Maybe, if there was something in it for Caleb.

⊷——⊷

When I returned home, Elise had already sent preliminary reports on Jess and Carla. Her internet must be working again.

I emailed back, thanking her, and added the bike rental guy, Barry Gates, to her list. I included the info from Edna's file on him.

Nothing I didn't already know in either of the reports she'd sent. This happened all too often, but the checks were still necessary. One didn't want to miss anything.

Carla's report included several previous addresses, going back to when she was still married to Caleb.

"I want to go talk to Carla's old neighbors," I told Will. "To eliminate her as a suspect," I added more vehemently.

"Maybe I should go. You're too close to this."

I shook my head. "I need to do it. Besides, people may be more likely to open up to a woman."

Will nodded, as rustling sounds came from the baby monitor on the breakfast bar. Noelle's morning naps were getting shorter.

He headed for the nursery.

I debated whether to take Buddy with me. He could be a distraction. But he was part of my protection—Will and I had trained him to do certain maneuvers that police dogs use. I'd also learned some self-defense tactics from YouTube videos.

Ms. Snark snickered.

Don't laugh. Those moves have saved me more than once.

I decided to err on the side of caution. "Come on, boy."

At Carla's old neighborhood, I knocked on three doors before getting an answer.

Two doors down from the Wilkes's old address, a short, round woman of a "certain age" stood in front of me. Wrinkled and with her hair dyed an unconvincing solid black, she could be anywhere from fifty to seventy.

She glanced down at Buddy but asked no questions. Probably not a dog person, but not afraid of them either.

I gave her the spiel I'd prepared, that I was a private investigator checking on Caleb Wilkes's background because he'd applied for an insurance policy for his new business. I was hoping she hadn't heard that he was dead.

"He's starting yet another business?" There was a slight sneer in her voice.

"Apparently so. The insurance company that hired me is run by a Christian man who likes to check on the character of applicants before he writes policies for them."

She gave me a funny look. "Is that legal?"

"It's not unusual for insurance companies to do background checks on applicants, for criminal histories and such." I shrugged. "Checking on other things is okay, as long as we don't break any privacy laws."

"But isn't that discrimination?"

Sheez Louise, is this woman a lawyer or something? Ms. Snark said internally.

Ignoring her, I gave the woman a smile. "He only wants to make sure the applicant isn't a truly nasty person."

The woman pursed her lips. "Well, I'm afraid that's exactly what Caleb Wilkes is." She leaned forward and whispered, "He beat his wife."

I faked a shocked expression. "He did?"

She nodded. "Or should I say, wives. Both Carla and Sheila, only Sheila had a better lawyer. She got the house when they divorced. Still lives there."

"So how do you know he beat them?" I asked, trying not to sound too eager.

"Because I was the one who usually called the police on him. I'd hear them screaming at each other from two houses over."

"But couldn't they just have been arguing loudly?"

She shook her head. "Carla would have bruises the next day, but she rarely pressed charges." She leaned forward again. "Until she grew a backbone. The last couple of times he started beatin' on her, she turned on him. Once she chased him out of the house with a baseball bat."

Despite this information indicating that Carla was capable of violence, I felt a sense of pride. *You go, girl!*

The woman paused, took a deep breath. "The second time, she marched him through the door at gunpoint, told him to get in his car and leave and never come back."

That *could very well be what prompted him to get a restraining order.*

"Did he come back?" I asked.

"Yeah, but only after she was gone. He hired a lawyer, and he eventually got the house in the property settlement. She packed up her stuff, yelled, 'Good riddance,' in the middle of the lawn, and drove away. I was a little afraid she'd burn the place down."

"She was that angry?"

She pursed her lips again. "Wouldn't you be, if your good-for-nothin' spouse gave you lung cancer with his secondhand smoke?"

CHAPTER SEVEN

I headed home with a heavy heart. Three other residents had corroborated the first woman's story, that Wilkes had beaten Carla, and that she'd finally fought back and had eventually divorced him, after she was diagnosed with cancer.

I decided to stop at the diner for a late lunch, and to check alibis. Duh, I should've done that first. If Carla had a good one, I could stop worrying about her.

Since Buddy was with me, we went around to the gazebo. It had warmed up some, now hovering in the high sixties. I claimed a table in the sun, settled Buddy under it, and went to tap on the kitchen door.

After a moment, Carla stuck her head out. "Hey, Marcia." Her voice was cheerful, but with a forced quality. With the boss in jail, it must be hard for the diner staff to keep up a good front.

"Hey, can I get a buffalo burger please," I said, "and a few minutes of your time when you can spare them."

She gave me a curious look, but nodded and disappeared back inside the building.

Ten minutes later, she brought out my burger. She set the plate in front of me, then sat down across the table.

"What's up?"

"Jess hired us, Will and me, to help her."

"I heard," Carla said. "If anybody can get to the bottom of this, you two can. Hey, we're collecting money to pay the bail bondsman's fee to get her out."

"How much is the bail? And thanks for the compliment."

"Twenty thousand, so we need two thousand to get her out."

"That's not very high bail for murder."

"Her lawyer got an immediate preliminary hearing, by pointing out that Jess owns a small business and is suffering great financial loss by being in jail. Johnny went and testified as a character witness. He didn't let on that they were a couple, just said that he'd known her as a respected member of the community for several years. He told me the prosecutor's case sounded shaky, and her attorney made a convincing argument that she has strong ties to the community and isn't a flight risk. The judge apparently agreed."

I pulled my wallet out of my jacket pocket and took out all the bills I had on me—a twenty and a ten. "Put the burger on my tab. Wish it could be more."

"S'okay. You're doing a lot for her already. And we're almost to goal now. Johnny started the pot with a thousand. It was what he'd been saving to buy her ring."

A lump formed in my throat.

"So, what do you need to ask me?" Carla said.

"Um…" I swallowed hard. "I need to check people's alibis.

The time-of-death window is ten p.m. Christmas evening to three a.m. the next morning."

Will had gotten that info from a buddy at the medical examiner's office. At ten that night, Caleb had told his wife he was feeling restless and was going to walk over to the bakery, maybe finish up a couple of tasks. Based on the degree of rigor mortis, he'd been dead at least eight hours when I'd found him.

Carla stared at me for a moment—a somewhat strange reaction, I thought.

"Jess hosted Christmas dinner at the farm," she finally said, "for the four of us. Then she and Johnny went for a drive, to check out the Christmas lights around the area. I had a headache, so Russ left, and I went to bed early."

"What time?"

"About nine-thirty. I took an aspirin and a sleeping pill and slept until six-thirty the next morning."

"Do you know when Johnny brought her home?"

Carla shook her head. "I didn't hear them come in. They both say he left around eleven."

Something didn't add up here. I'd seen Jess at the diner at nine, and she'd been alone.

And Carla had a funny look on her face.

"They *said* that, but you're not sure you believe them?" I asked.

She sighed. "I thought I heard a car engine out front, as I was waking up."

"Couldn't that have been Jess leaving for the diner?"

She shook her head again. "She leaves at five-thirty, to have time to bake fresh biscuits before she opens at seven."

"Did you tell Detective Brown about the car?"

Carla glared at me. "No. And if you tell him, I'll deny it."

I was about to ask her why Johnny and Jess would've lied about spending the night together, especially since that would give Jess an alibi.

But Carla jumped up. "I gotta get back in there. It's not fair to Lisa to leave her on her own this long."

"Of course," I said, but I was talking to her back, as she strode toward the kitchen door.

⊷——⊶

I ended up feeding Buddy half my burger. I'd lost my appetite.

I texted Will to see how he was doing with the baby. *Everything okay?*

Yup. We're fine.

Mind if I stay out a little longer?

No problem.

I meandered around Mayfair, Buddy at my side, trying to sort out what I'd learned.

But all I came up with were more questions. If Johnny and Jess had taken a drive all evening, then why was Jess alone at the diner at nine, smacking around a clump of dough? And at what time had Johnny picked her up again and taken her home—before or after ten p.m., the last time Caleb was seen alive?

And what was with the two of them keeping it from the detective that he was her alibi for the rest of the night?

Carla's alibi wasn't completely solid either. If she was lying about the sleeping pill, she could've gone out in the middle of the night, without Jess's or Johnny's knowledge.

What should I do next?

I certainly didn't want to tell Joe Brown what I'd found out from Carla's neighbors. Although it wouldn't be hard for him to discover, if he bothered to do some research on her. But as far as I knew, the detective wasn't even looking at anyone but Jess.

I wasn't even sure I should tell Will. As former law enforcement, he might feel obligated to tell Brown or the sheriff. But it had been a long time since I'd kept secrets from him.

One, it's not good for a marriage, and two, every time I had kept something from him, it had blown up in my face.

And it probably will this time. I threw my hands up in the air, startling Buddy.

He'd originally been trained as a service dog for a PTSD-suffering Marine, so he did what he'd been trained to do—leaned against my leg, grounding me with his solid presence. He whined, a suggestion that I pet him to further reduce my anxiety.

I sighed and patted his head. "Thanks, boy."

"Hey, Marcia."

I glanced up. I'd come around full circle and was back on my own street. And my neighbor Sherie was waving from her front porch.

We strolled up her walkway.

She gave me an apprising once-over. "Why so glum, child?"

I shook my head. "I can't talk about it. Related to a case."

She nodded and gestured for me to come up on the porch. "Come sit with me for a spell, tell me how the family's doing."

She pointed to the well-padded glider at one end of her porch. I dutifully sat, and she went inside for some iced tea. Buddy settled at my feet.

I admired the plants hanging from the porch roof. They were her pride and joy. She fussed over them every day, and they responded with lush foliage and colorful flowers, even this time of year.

If they were mine, I'd forget to bring them in when there was a frost and they'd all be dead.

You really are a Gloomy Gus today, aren't you? Ms. Snark observed internally.

I ignored her as Sherie returned with a tray. I jumped up to hold the screen door open for her. The tray held two tall glasses of tea, plus a sugar bowl and spoon for me. Knowing that I'd never developed a taste for Southern sweet tea, Sherie kept a pitcher of unsweetened tea in her fridge, just for me.

Her thoughtfulness always made me smile, but today the smile was a little weak.

"You sure you can't tell me what's bothering you?" Sherie asked, as she set the tray on a small wicker table.

I shook my head again and doctored my tea with one teaspoon of sugar. "Distract me with other things," I said.

And so she did, telling me about her youngest daughter Sybil, whom I knew well. Sybil had been in her late teens and still living at home when I'd moved to Mayfair. Then she'd returned to stay with her mom during the pandemic, and she and I had gotten into a bit of hot water together, trying to find out if one of my clients was being held against his will at a mental health facility.

That same client was now Carla's boyfriend.

"Sybil's finally found her niche as a nurse," Sherie was saying. "She's working for a pediatrician, helping with patients, and she's pursuing the extra training to become a nurse practitioner."

That news cheered me some, although not as much as it should have.

Again, Sherie gave me a look that was one part worry and

one part sympathy.

I sighed. "Let's just say that the case isn't going in a good direction." I paused, gave some thought to what was really bothering me. "And people I thought I knew well are not telling the truth, or at least, not the whole truth."

"Jess's case?" Sherie asked.

My head jerked around, my surprised expression giving her the answer.

She patted my knee. "Don't worry. You know I'll keep things to myself."

I let out another sigh. Could I tell her? No... Even putting aside the whole confidentiality thing, it would only have her worrying too—which would do no good.

Instead, I said, "I guess I'm wondering if I'm really cut out to be a detective. I'm stuck in this investigation." I really wasn't, but I didn't want to go where the evidence was pointing. "And I'm not sure I have the stomach for digging up dirt on people."

"Well first," Sherie said, "let me tell you that I think you are a natural detective. You've stuck your nose in everything that's gone wrong in this town since you moved here, and you've played a role in solving those mysteries. Plus all the times you've gone to bat for your veteran clients who've gotten into trouble."

I mustered a smile. "Thanks."

"If you're stuck right now, you need to wait until the next move comes to you. It will. Girl, you need to learn some patience."

I snorted softly. "That's never been my strongest suit."

"Except with your dogs," she pointed out. "Apply the same thing here. When you're training, you know the animals will get it eventually. So trust that *you* will get it eventually and just keeping plugging along."

I nodded acknowledgment of the sound advice and took a sip of tea.

"As for digging up dirt on people," she continued, "if there's dirt there to be found, that's not your fault. It's on them."

"True," I said. "But sometimes good people have bad things in their histories, things they didn't have complete control over. I don't like to be the one who digs up those skeletons."

"But sometimes they need to come to light." Sherie gave me an intense look. "Remember the real skeleton that got dug up? If you and Will hadn't kept digging, figuratively speaking, Susanna wouldn't be with us today."

"Also true." I spent a moment reliving the shock of finding Susanna in a long-term care facility, where her father had committed her decades before, believing she was incurably depressed. He'd told the rest of the family that she'd died, perhaps thinking that would be an easier grief to get past. And then he'd died himself shortly after that.

"That was painful for Edna at the time," Sherie was saying, "but she ended up with her precious niece back."

"It was painful for you too," I said.

"Yes, it was, but I got my childhood friend back in the end." She paused, sipped tea. "And it's a good lesson about secrets tending to cause more problems than they solve."

A stab of guilt in my chest. But I couldn't tell Will—not yet, at least.

I gulped down the last of my iced tea and set the empty glass on the tray. I patted Sherie's hand. "Thanks for the pep talk. It helped."

She gave me a warm smile. "Any time, child."

Buddy and I descended from the porch. I waved over my

shoulder and we walked to the street. But I didn't turn us left toward our own walkway.

I turned right, back toward the center of town—to track down Johnny Redmond.

CHAPTER EIGHT

I found Johnny in his cruiser toward the end of Mayfair Avenue. He was sitting, idling, on the side of the road. As I approached, I saw that he was on his cell phone.

He spotted me, said a few words, and disconnected. His window whirred down.

"Hey, Marcia."

"Hey, Johnny," I called out cheerfully. Then, in a lower, more sober voice, added, "We need to talk."

His face fell. He jerked his head toward his passenger door. "Get in."

I jogged around the car, tucked Buddy into the backseat, and got in the front.

Johnny drove a few hundred feet to the junction with Highway 25 and turned right. Mid-afternoon on a weekday between Christmas and New Year's, the country road was deserted.

Nothing stirred except the palmetto bushes along the sides, ruffled by a slight breeze.

I opened my mouth, but Johnny spoke first. "That rubber glove you found…"

"Yes."

"Good news is the lab could lift a print from inside it, bad news is it wasn't in the system."

"So whoever was wearing the glove doesn't have a criminal record."

Johnny nodded. "And it wasn't Jess's."

I bit the inside of my cheek to keep from asking if they'd checked it against Carla's prints.

"What about on the murder weapon, that board they found," I said. "Any prints on that?"

"Nothing useful. Only smudges, but it is Wilkes's blood type. They're still waiting on the DNA testing on that."

Johnny sighed. "More bad news, and you gotta keep this to yourself. There were some clothes in the dumpster. Loose fitting fleece pants and a long-sleeved tee shirt, size of an average woman. With paint smears on them. And there were a couple of dark hairs on the shirt. Lab sent them out for DNA testing as well." He paused, eyes on the road, and swallowed hard. "And they sent some of Jess's hair, for comparison."

My heart had fallen into my stomach at the words, *paint smears*. Now it lay there, a lump of dread. I didn't have to ask the colors of the clothing. I was pretty sure they were the black pants and dark green tee I'd lent Carla.

And now my questions for Johnny were that much more pressing.

"Carla tells me you and Jess took a drive after dinner on

Christmas, and you weren't back by the time she went to bed at nine-thirty." I paused, waiting for some reaction from Johnny.

And got none. He stared out the windshield at the road ahead.

"There's just one problem," I continued. "I spoke to Jess at the diner around nine. She was by herself and pretty upset that Wilkes was throwing a grand opening gala the same day as her big dinner."

Still no reaction other than a slight clenching of his jaw.

"Where were you then?" I asked.

"If you must know," he ground out the words, eyes still fixated on the road, "I was running around town, pulling down that creep's notices about his gala. Then I went back to the diner and took Jess home."

I'd never seen Johnny angry before. Usually, he was pretty laid back. Could *he* have been angry enough to go after Caleb with a board?

"What time did you get back to Jess's house?" I asked.

"Around ten, I guess."

Hmmm, Ms. Snark commented internally.

Yeah, the timing is tight.

"I'm not sure how to word this discreetly," I said, "so I'm just gonna blurt it out. Did you spend the night with Jess that night?"

Johnny's cheeks flushed. I thought he wasn't going to answer, but finally he said, "Yes, but Jess wouldn't let me tell anybody."

I shook my head. "Why not? I mean, sure, this is a small town, but most folks aren't prudish. Will and I lived together for almost two years before we got married."

"That wasn't why." Johnny glanced my way, then back at the road. "Jess was worried about what it might do to my career if it came out that I was in a serious relationship with a suspect."

"So you let her be arrested?" I said, incredulous.

"No. This was before, when Detective Brown was first asking them for alibis. Jess said we should pretend that I left the night before. She thought that she and Carla could alibi each other."

He paused, sucked in air. "But Carla said she'd taken a sleeping pill, and Brown figures that cancels out her alibiing Jess."

I heaved a sigh. "Which it does."

"But we'd already lied by then. Now Jess won't let me tell the truth because the lying would definitely doom my chances of making sergeant."

"Sergeant?"

"I took the exam in November and did well on it. Promotions are going to be announced the first of the year. I'm hoping...I *was* hoping..." He trailed off and veered into a farmer's lane.

Slamming the cruiser into park, he pulled his phone out. "I'm going to call Brown now and tell him the truth. He'll have to let Jess go."

My chest tightened. *And then he'll turn his sights on Carla.* Ignoring the lump of dread in my stomach, I nodded encouragement.

Johnny said very little on his end, once he'd explained where he'd been on Christmas night. Only several "yeah, but's." Finally, he spluttered, "But, but..." He lowered the phone and turned to me, his broad face pale and sagging.

"He doesn't believe me. He thinks I'm only trying to rescue my girl."

⊷⊷

Johnny dropped us off at the end of Mayfair Avenue. It was

four-thirty, close enough to dinner time. In no mood to cook, I walked to the diner to get food for tonight. We'd reheat it later.

Lisa—who'd been waiting tables for Jess for years—was silhouetted in the front window, delivering plates to a table with two elderly couples. I waited for her to lift her head, then waved and gestured to the side, indicating I'd be around back with Buddy.

We settled at one of the picnic tables in the gazebo.

Lisa came out a couple of minutes later. "Hey, Marcia. Did y'all have a good Christmas?"

"We did," I faked cheerfulness. "And you?"

"It was great. Such fun watching the kids open their presents. What can I get you?"

"Two meatloaf dinners to go, please."

Noelle was mostly eating table food now. I would mush together some meatloaf, mashed potatoes, and bits of green beans for her. Of course, even if I spooned it into her mouth, she'd end up with some of it smeared all over her face. I smiled a little at the mental image.

"Did Jess get bailed out yet?" I asked Lisa.

She nodded. "We only needed forty dollars more, so we took it out of the tip jar for today. She and Carla got back a few minutes ago."

"Can you ask Jess to come out for a sec?"

Lisa was back in less than two minutes. "Uh, your food will be ready soon," she said, in a hesitant voice, her expression confused. "But Jess said...she said I should just tell you that she's talked to Johnny."

Ten minutes later, I was trudging home with the plastic bag

of food, my chest aching and my stomach twisted in a knot. My mojo was definitely off today. I'd set out to clear my friends of murder, and not only had I failed miserably at that, I'd manage to piss one of them off.

And my bad mojo day wasn't done with me yet. My phone pinged as we turned onto my walkway. It was a text from Carla.

Got a call from my old neighbor. Thanks for stirring the pot. Stay out of my business.

I groaned and plopped down on my porch steps. Buddy gave me a worried look before settling at my feet.

I hadn't liked Carla when I'd first met her. She had a prickly personality, to put it mildly. But she'd mellowed as I'd gotten to know her. Or maybe she'd gotten less prickly because she'd come to trust me, think of me as a friend.

But prickly was back. How had I managed to alienate two friends in one day, when I'd only been trying to help?

I stayed on the porch steps, staring into space, until the cold from the cement soaked through my jeans.

⊷—⊶

Whimpers from the baby monitor woke me the next morning. Noelle rarely full-out cries, but if we don't respond to the whimpers, eventually she will.

I opened one eye. Will was already out of bed, looking lean and handsome in his white tee shirt and beltless jeans hanging loose on narrow hips.

"I got her," he said. "Go back to sleep."

I smiled and snuggled down into my pillow again, thinking how a man being an attentive father is somehow sexy.

Then memories of the previous day came flooding back. I shivered, despite the warm nest of bedding.

No point in trying to get back to sleep now.

The sound of Will's voice came through the monitor. "What's up, baby girl?"

My heart warmed in my chest. At least I had my little family, even if my list of friends was dwindling.

Friends! I knew what else would cheer me up. I felt around for my phone on the bedside table and called my bestie.

"Good morning, Sunshine," Becky's perpetually cheerful voice greeted me.

"Hey there, is this a good time to talk?"

A short chuckle. "As good as any. The twins are currently playing with their new toys next to the Christmas tree."

With a knot in my stomach, I blurted out, "I have a confession to make."

"Oh, that sounds ominous," she said, but her voice lost none of its cheery tone. It took a lot to bring Becky down. Only once had I seen her truly depressed, and that was when one of the twins was missing!

I took a deep breath and filled her in on recent events in Mayfair.

"So where's the confession in all that?" she asked.

"As with any case, we did background checks on everyone concerned, and I found out something about one of my friends here in town, and I checked it out." I was trying not to get too specific, for the sake of confidentiality. Plus, Becky came to Mayfair to visit fairly often. It would be awkward for her to interact with Jess and Carla if she knew too much about their personal lives.

"And…?" Becky said.

"And she got wind of it and is now mad at me." Another deep breath. I rushed on. "Then I followed up on something she told me about someone else, and that set something off…" This being vague thing was harder than it looked. "And that other person is also now mad at me."

"I take it that one of these people is Jess Randall, the one who got arrested?"

"Yes," I admitted, after a moment's hesitation.

"And she's mad at you for doing your job and trying to clear her? That's crazy."

The knot in my stomach loosened some. "Thanks for the validation that she's overreacting, but–"

"It's probably because she was already uptight," Becky said, now playing devil's advocate. "Who wouldn't be in her shoes?"

"Yeah, and…well, I did something, or rather I encouraged someone else to do something that she didn't want them to do."

The sound of a sigh—it sounded like a frustrated one. But was she frustrated with my vagueness or with Jess?

"What would've happened if you hadn't butted in?" she asked. "Did it make a difference in the case, move things toward resolving anything?"

My turn to blow out a sigh. "Not really. I found out that Jess has an alibi, but that blinkety-blank detective doesn't believe the person she was with."

And now Johnny's career was in jeopardy. I didn't tell Becky that part.

"Here's what I'm thinking," she said, "maybe you should cool it for now with those two, Jess and the other one. Maybe check out other people involved, like the wife and the business partner."

"Hmm, as of yesterday, I hadn't heard back from Elise on

their background checks. But maybe she's sent them by now."

"Well, go check, girl!" Screeching children's voices in the background. "Oops, gotta go. Suddenly they both want the same toy. Time for Mediator Mommy."

I pictured my adorable godchildren—now four—in my mind's eye, their smooth cream-colored skin, big brown eyes, and dark curls so like their mother's. Winston getting tall and lanky like his father. Jasmine a bit shorter, her face soft and more round.

My heart warmed in my chest as I disconnected…and realized that Becky's cheerful, practical approach had rubbed off on me. Plus, I now had a course of action.

I jumped out of bed and threw on yesterday's clothes.

Out in the study, I booted up my laptop on my desk, and brought up my email program. Sure enough, there were two emails from Elise, with attachments. The first was on Dee Wilkes, née Delores Gibson. I skimmed it. Nothing all that interesting, other than a previous marriage.

I was opening the second report, on Leroy Jenkins, when a hand appeared next to my shoulder. I jumped.

"Sorry, didn't mean to startle you." Will's hand held a cup of coffee. Noelle was balanced on his other hip.

I took the cup gratefully. "Sorry I'm so jumpy. I'll take her now and feed her breakfast."

"Already done, while you were on the phone with Becky."

"Oh." I felt heat creeping up my cheeks. Now I could add crappy mother to crappy friend.

Will narrowed his eyes in a concerned look. "What's up, Marcia?"

I turned toward him, opened my mouth—then something I'd seen in my peripheral vision registered.

I turned back to the report. Halfway down was a subheading, in bold: ***Criminal Charges***.

"Guess what?" I said to Will, instead of the answer I'd been about to give him. "Caleb Wilkes's partner has a record, for perjury and accessory to fraud."

CHAPTER NINE

Will and I good-naturedly debated who should go talk to Leroy Jenkins. "He might be more forthcoming with me," I pointed out. "You're not with the sheriff's department anymore, but you still might represent 'The Man' to him." I made air quotes.

Will sighed. "You're probably right. Okay, but call me when you get there and leave the line open."

"Good idea." We called it our poor man's wire.

I headed for the bedroom for a shower and fresh clothes.

Fifteen minutes later, I was strolling along the boardwalk in front of the new buildings, Buddy at my side. The air temperature was high sixties, so I'd donned a lightweight cardigan over my red camp shirt, one of the ones Edna had made for me when I was pregnant. It was too big now—except around my hips, sadly. But it and its siblings were the only shirts I owned with breast pockets. I had called Will, and my phone now rested in one of those pockets, the line open.

The front door of the bakery was locked, and I didn't see any-one inside when I peeked through the plate-glass window.

Hmm, I'd thought about talking to the bike rental guy after Leroy, but I could go there first.

"No Leroy at the bakery yet," I said out loud for Will's ben-efit. "I'm going to go check on something else and come back."

"What something else?" Will's voice was muffled by the cloth of the pocket.

"The bike rental guy." I'd reached the end of the boardwalk and was staring at the bikes, in neat rows, with metal cords lock-ing them together.

A grunt from Will as the door of the shop opened.

"Shh," I whispered.

A man stepped out onto the boardwalk. He was indeed an aging hippie, on the heavy side, with a receding hairline in front and a long, graying ponytail hanging down his back.

And his red flannel shirt and baggy jeans definitely smelled of marijuana smoke.

"Can I help you?" he said in a pleasant baritone.

"I was just admiring your bikes. I'm Marcia Banks-Haines. I live over there." I gestured toward my house, barely visible beyond the pasture fencing and barn. I didn't offer my hand, not wanting to get too close to this unknown guy.

"I'm Barry Gates." He didn't offer his hand either. What did that mean? Maybe nothing. Considering his age, he might've been raised to wait for the woman to initiate a handshake.

I pointed to the bikes. "That's a lot of 'em. Do you think we'll get that many tourists at any given time?"

"Well, eventually maybe half that many," he said. "Some of

the bikes are for sale rather than rental."

"Oh, that's a good idea. I may buy one myself, to get around town. And get my exercise while I'm at it." I didn't tell him that I already got plenty of that chasing after Noelle, mucking stalls, and walking dogs. "Uh, can I offer some advice about your business?"

"Sure." He gave me a small smile.

I had no idea what the smile meant, but I forged ahead. "You may not notice it because you're used to the smell, but it's obvious you use marijuana."

The smile faded and his eyes went hard. "Yeah. What of it?"

"Well, I don't care, but some people in town might."

"It's legal now in Florida." His tone was borderline belligerent.

"For medicinal purposes. Do you have a medical card?"

"Um, not yet. Been meaning to get one, but with setting up the shop and all…" He trailed off, looked away. "I've got a bad back. The weed is for the pain."

"Well, the odor's pretty obvious. I smelled it the other day as well, when I walked past the door. Could be bad for business, and someone might report you."

His shoulders hunched up and he took a step toward me. "Someone like you?" He wasn't much taller than me, but he'd puffed out his chest. Was that unconscious or was he intentionally trying to seem menacing?

Growling, Buddy inserted himself between us, the hair standing up on his neck.

The guy stepped back.

I held out my hand toward my dog in the *wait* signal. "Nope," I said, keeping my voice light. "Like I said, I don't care."

I paused, then added, "I'm surprised none of the other shopkeepers have picked up on the smell."

He shook his head. "Nobody's said anything."

"I heard you and Caleb Wilkes were chatting a few days ago." I'd heard no such thing. I was fishing. "He didn't catch a whiff of it?"

"Who told you that?" The semi-belligerent tone was back.

I shrugged. "I don't recall now. People have been talking a lot about him recently, you know, after he…" I trailed off, watching the guy's face carefully.

His gaze flicked away for a moment, then he was looking over my shoulder instead of making eye contact. "Yeah, that was pretty creepy. But I heard they arrested the diner owner for it."

I shrugged again and pushed a little. "Caleb didn't say anything about the weed smell, when you were talking to him?"

"Nah, we were just shootin' the breeze for a couple of minutes." He let out a chuckle that didn't sound all that genuine.

"Okay, well, I'll think about buying a bike. Good luck with the shop." I turned, keeping Buddy between us and headed back the way we'd come.

"Thanks," he called out from behind me, half a beat late.

When we were two buildings away from the bike shop, I said to Will, "Did you get all that?"

"Most of it," came from my pocket. "He sounded kind of gruff."

"He looked even gruffer," I said as we approached the bakery again. "I'll fill you in on him when I get home."

The bakery door now stood open, letting in the cool breeze. I understood why when I stepped inside. Heat was radiating from the curtained opening that led to the kitchen—along with a delectable fragrance that almost cancelled out the fresh paint smell.

I squinted at the wall and could barely make out vague outlines of the symbols and words that had been scrawled there. But someone who didn't know about the graffiti probably wouldn't notice, especially once the white shelves attached high on that wall were filled with baked goods.

Three small white wooden tables, surrounded by matching chairs, were lined up against the lower part of the wall.

"In case customers want to sit and enjoy my baking here."

I jumped and twisted around.

Leroy was in the opening to the kitchen, holding the curtain to one side. Buddy had inserted himself between us, but he didn't growl.

"What's cooking?" I mustered a smile. I really needed to get my nerves under control.

"Two pies and a batch of cookies. I'm testing out the new oven, to see if it runs hot or cold. So far, it's leaning toward hot. I burned the first pan of cookies."

I sniffed the air. Sure enough, there was a slight burnt smell under the more delicious aromas.

"Have a seat. The second pan is almost done." He gave me a big smile. "I'll bring some out for you to taste-test."

"That sounds wonderful." I settled at one of the tables, Buddy at my feet.

Leroy was back in a few minutes with a plate of cookies in one hand and two steaming white china mugs in the other. He deposited them carefully on the table. "I figured coffee would also be a good idea."

"You figured right."

"Does your dog need some water?"

"No, but thanks for asking."

"Give the cookies a minute to cool." Leroy sat back in his chair and took a sip of coffee. "Are you just out for a walk or did you have something to ask me?"

I gave him a startled look.

"Word travels fast in this town. I heard you were working to clear Jess, you and your husband."

"You're on a first name basis with her now?" I studied his light brown face. It was wrinkle-free, and the fashionable stubble on his cheeks and chin was dark. No older than thirty-five would be my guess.

"Of course. We're neighbors, aren't we?" he said. "I don't share Caleb's competitive nature, never did."

Okay, time to get down to business. But first I grabbed a cookie, in case he snatched them back if things got heated.

It practically melted in my mouth. "Oh my," I mumbled around it. "That's *so* good."

Leroy smiled. "That's what the shelves are for. Mostly they'll hold cookie boxes. Chocolate chip," he gestured toward the plate, "is my specialty, but I make a mean oatmeal raisin too."

"Will's favorite." I paused, licked the chocolate off my lips. "And yes, he and I are investigating Caleb's death, to try to clear Jess. As part of that, we did background checks on all concerned parties. And–"

"And you found my criminal record." He was still leaning back, nonchalant, but his eyes had hardened some. "That was my brother's doing…or half-brother actually, but we were raised together. I always looked up to him, so when he asked me to testify in his slip-and-fall suit against a grocery store, of course I said yes. I told what I thought was the truth, that he'd been complaining of pain ever since he'd taken a tumble in their produce department." Leroy paused, leaned forward. "He'd even been to a chiropractor, who also testified, and he was walking around in a back brace for a couple of months."

He shook his head. "I really felt bad for Rick. He'd always been a bit of a health nut, exercised regularly, ate right. To see him in pain like that, and not able to do the things he loved." He paused, stared off into space.

"What things?" I asked.

Leroy snorted. "The things that did him in. Unbeknownst to Rick, the insurance company had hired a PI, like y'all." He waved his hand in my direction. "The PI kept following him around even after the trial. Three days later, he followed him to a tributary of the St. John's River. He took a video of Rick taking off the brace, doing some stretches with a big smile on his face, and then hauling a kayak out of the back of his pickup. He had a camper cap on it and had apparently loaded it up while inside his garage."

He sighed. "The assistant state's attorney was pissed, said we'd made a mockery of the court system. She threw the book at Rick, and also charged me and the chiropractor as accessories. I tried to tell her that I'd been fooled too, that I had no idea he was okay, but she didn't believe me, and neither did the jury."

This time, I let the silence stretch out for a while—long enough for me to eat another cookie. "Have you seen your brother recently?"

He shook his head again. "All this was ten years ago. I was only twenty. I did two years of a four-year sentence and got parole for good behavior. One of the conditions was that I'd stay away from him. He got eight years and a big fine, served four of them. By the time my parole was up, he was out and we'd lost touch."

He shrugged. "Probably for the best," he said, but the corners of his mouth drooped.

Back at the house, Noelle was down for her morning nap, although how long that would last was debatable.

Leroy had boxed up the cookies and insisted I take them with me. Will and I sat at the breakfast bar and shared them, while I reported on what Leroy had said and filled him in on Barry Gates, aka the Bike Guy.

By the time I had finished, rustling noises were coming from the baby monitor. Yeah, her morning nap was gonna be history real soon.

"This Gates fella," Will said, "we can check him out some more, once Elise reports back on him."

I nodded. "Look, this is your week off. Lemme take over with Noelle, and you…" I trailed off. Will didn't really have any hobbies, other than renovating things, and the house had now been completely redone. "…you do you," I finished lamely.

"I do have a new book to read." He mentioned an adventure author I'd never heard of—I'm a mystery reader, all the way.

"I'm going to take Noelle for a walk, so you can have some peace and quiet for a while."

He let out a sigh. "Sounds like a plan."

Whimpering was threatening to turn into a full-blown wail when I entered the nursery. Noelle sat up in her crib and gave me a big smile.

You are such a little con artist.

I put a finger inside the waistband of her tiny corduroy pants and the top edge of her diaper and peeked inside the latter. Still dry and clean. "Come on, little one." I scooped her up.

Fifteen minutes later—nothing is ever quick when dealing

with a one-year-old—we were ready to go, with Noelle bundled up and strapped in her carrier. I'd put the puppy in the back-yard to run around for a while, so Will wouldn't have to worry about him.

At the front door, I stopped, looked at Buddy lying on his bed under the picture window. "You coming?"

He raised his head but didn't get up.

A vise squeezed my heart. He was getting so old, the gray on his snout now hard to ignore.

"Okay, you rest, boy. We'll be back soon."

Outside, I snapped the baby carrier into its stroller base and pointed us toward Edna's motel and the diner. I took a deep breath. Yes, we had a murder to solve, but there were potential leads now, other than Carla or Jess. Maybe someone from Leroy's past had come searching for him, and had run into Caleb, his business partner, instead.

And regardless of the drama going on in town right now, *my* life was good. My child was healthy and happy, and our new PI agency was off to a good start.

Carla and Jess would eventually get over being mad at me, especially if we cleared them of suspicion. *And* I lived in central Florida where a slight dip below sixty-five degrees was consid-ered a cold day in the winter.

The new year is gonna be a good one, I thought, taking another deep breath of the cool, fresh air and letting a sense of content-ment envelope me.

A loud crack.

What the H...? Had a car backfired?

No, dummy. Such a cliché, Ms. Snark scoffed.

Another sharp crack.

Heart pounding, I raced toward the diner. I had to get Noelle off the street!

CHAPTER TEN

At the front of the diner, I hesitated. What if the shots had come from in there?

The plate-glass windows reflected the sun into my face. All I could make out were shadowy movements inside. I turned the stroller and raced for the corner of the building. I'd go in the back, where I could see through the window in the kitchen door, *before* making my presence known.

As I rounded the corner, another sharp crack. I jumped.

Noelle was fussing. I quickly unstrapped her, grabbed her up, and ran the last few steps. Crouching under the window in the diner's back door, I peeked inside.

Lisa was huddled under the big metal worktable, her phone to her ear. She spotted me and waved frantically for me to come in.

The door was unlocked. I went in low, bent over the baby in a protective hunch.

"Lock the door!" Lisa yelled.

I pivoted and grabbed the knob, twisted the lock—not that it would stop anybody for long. All they'd have to do was break the window and reach in to unlock it.

I scrambled under the table, sat cross-legged, and lowered Noelle to my lap. She stared up at me wide-eyed.

I struggled to slow my breathing before I hyperventilated, telling my brain—which kept screaming *active shooter!* internally—to shut up.

"The shots didn't come from in here, then?" My voice was more than a little shaky.

Lisa shook her head. "No. I couldn't really tell which direction they were coming from."

"I think that last one was from the shops' area."

Or the barn maybe? My heart stuttered in my chest. *Niña!*

"That was Johnny on the phone," Lisa said. "We're to sit tight while he checks around town. After the first two shots, Jess herded the customers into the restrooms. No windows and the doors lock from the inside. I locked the front door and was running to lock the back one, when the third shot…" She trailed off, shuddering. "I scooted under here."

I quickly looked around. "Not sure this is the best spot." The table would save us if the shooter was hanging from the ceiling, but we could be seen from both the back door and the doors into the dining area.

"Over there." Lisa pointed to another table—smaller but also metal—along one wall. She crawled out and raced over to it, shoved the few things on it to the floor and tried to tip it over. It was too heavy.

I'd wiggled out from under the bigger table. Awkwardly,

while holding Noelle tight against me, I scrambled to my feet and ran to Lisa.

I sat Noelle against the wall. "Stay put." And Lisa and I managed to tip the table on its side.

But of course, Noelle had not stayed put. She was on her hands and knees, headed across the kitchen. I scooped her up.

She let out a squawk of protest, which I ignored, and in a second we were once again huddled on the floor, now *behind* a metal barrier instead of under one. I tried not to think about whether or not the metal was thick enough to stop a bullet.

My phone beeped—from across the room. No doubt a text from Will, but apparently the phone had slipped out of my pocket as I was scrambling out from under the other table.

Minutes ticked by, fifteen of them. Silence from the front of the diner. Silence from outside the building. The only sound my phone, beeping several more times.

My stomach was queasy, thinking about Will. He must be frantic with worry. And Noelle was getting quite restless.

Rapping against the back door's window made Lisa and me jump. She stuck her head out. "It's Will."

I blew out pent-up air, as Lisa jumped up and went over to let him in.

"Have you seen–" He broke off when he spotted me, now standing beside the table, Noelle braced on my hip. He closed the space in two long strides and gave us a group hug.

"What's happening?" Lisa and I asked in unison.

"Nothing," Will said. He broke the hug, but kept an arm slung over my shoulders, his hand on Noelle's back. "And that's kinda scary. Johnny and I have been searching the town. We can't find anybody who might have fired those shots, and nobody saw anything helpful."

"I thought the last one might've come from the shops or the barn," I said.

He nodded. "I ran to the front of the house after the first two. I thought the third one came from the shops as well. We searched there first. They're all empty, except the bakery. Leroy was hiding in the kitchen. Claims he doesn't even own a gun."

He stopped, took a breath, then looked down at me, love and worry in his eyes. "I didn't know where you were, and when I got no answer to my texts…"

"I lost my phone," I said.

He nodded again. "Johnny said the diner was locked down. I figured you were in here, when I saw the stroller outside."

He reached out for Noelle. "Let me take her."

I didn't resist. She was getting heavy.

"Three deputies arrived a few minutes ago," he said. "They're helping Johnny do another circuit of the town. And they're going to search the shops, if they can find the owners. Leroy already said we could search the bakery, but we didn't take the time before. We needed to check out the rest of the town."

Crapola! Then Leroy would've had time to hide a gun or toss it, if he was the culprit. But why would he randomly start shooting?

Seems to be a thing lately, Ms. Snark commented internally, *to shoot up things and people for no good reason.*

I shuddered.

"Maybe it was just somebody target practicing in their backyard," Lisa said, her voice more anxious than hopeful.

Will gave her a skeptical look. I shared his skepticism. No one in Mayfair would do that so close to their neighbors' houses.

They'd go across Highway 25 to the homemade firing range Bill Baker had set up in the woods, next to a small hill that acted as the backstop for stray bullets.

Was it one of the newcomers? I thought but didn't say out loud. I didn't want to promote the idea that we should be wary of strangers—and always blame them when something bad happened. That might be the attitude in many small towns, but that wasn't Mayfair.

But it might be what Mayfair becomes, Ms. Snark pointed out, her tone more grim than snarky.

———

Will was subdued over our lunch of Mom's leftover chicken and veggie soup, pulled out of the freezer and microwaved. Noelle was contained in her highchair, happily mooshing the soft veggies I'd fished out of the soup for her and then jamming the mess into her mouth.

I was trying to figure out how to bring up my earlier concerns—that all this crime here in town would somehow change Mayfair.

"I got another call," Will said, "from that guy who's claiming I hit him."

"Oh?"

"I didn't answer, but he left a message, says he's getting a lawyer and is going to sue."

My stomach clenched. "Still no idea who he is?"

"No. He sent the photo he claimed he took of me driving away. It's definitely my truck, but you can't see any background, only darkness around it. Can't even tell if the truck is moving or not." He sighed.

"This guy's beginning to get on my nerves." He'd gone for a nonchalant tone, but there was an undercurrent of worry.

He shook his head, as if to clear it. "On another subject, that clown I'd been watching, the one who went for an evening run. Elise dug deeper, and it turns out he may be living under a false name. His driver's license had checked out as legit when she ran the first check on him. But this time, she contacted the town listed on his birth certificate, and they've got no record of him being born there."

"Hmm, interesting. Either the records got lost somehow, or the birth certificate was forged, then used to get a license."

He nodded.

"So," I said, "probably not somebody just trying to take advantage, after a real car crash."

"No. It's more likely he's a repeat offender, a true con man."

"Wasn't he hit from behind, when he stopped suddenly?"

"Yup. Claimed a cat had run across in front of him. The accident was ruled the other driver's fault, since you're supposed to leave enough room between you and the car in front, in case they suddenly stop."

"But people often leave too little space," I said. "Hey, does this mean we get that bonus from the insurance company?"

Will nodded again, but despite that happy thought, he stared glumly at his soup.

He looked as depressed as I felt. Con men, random shooters, not to mention a murderer. The world seemed to be coming apart all around us. *And here I'd been feeling so optimistic earlier, about the new year.*

Our conversation reminded me of Leroy's involvement in a

similar insurance fraud case. "Hey, is there a way to find out if Leroy Jenkins made any enemies in prison?"

"Already thought of that. Elise is digging deeper and I put in a call to one of the guards I know at the state penitentiary, to see if he knows anything about the guy."

I nodded, deciding to keep my concerns about Mayfair's atmosphere to myself. He didn't need any more pressure. And the fastest way to get the town back to normal was to solve Caleb Wilkes's murder.

You've also conveniently neglected to tell him, Ms. Snark pointed out, *about the clothes you lent to Carla, which ended up in a dumpster with paint on them.*

I keep forgetting.

Uh-huh. You could tell him now.

But I didn't. Instead, I said, "Elise's report on Dee Wilkes said she's been married before. Maybe we should talk to her ex."

"Yeah. I'll see if I can track him down this afternoon." Will didn't sound all that excited about the idea.

"I should do it. This is your week off."

"Not anymore. Someone shooting up my town has dampened my desire to kick back and relax."

"You think the shooting is related to the murder?"

He said nothing, just stared at me.

"Okay," I said, "it would be a bit of a coincidence if it's *not* related, and you…"

"…don't believe in coincidences," we said in unison.

After lunch, Will left to track down Dee Wilkes's ex. As soon as he was out the door, I texted Carla.

I know you're mad at me but I need to know what happened to the clothes I lent you.

No response.

She should still be home. It wasn't time yet for her shift at the diner. Maybe she was in the shower.

My phone beeped, right as Noelle started banging on her high-chair tray—her signal that she was ready to get down.

Wielding a damp cloth to wipe her hands and face with one hand, I checked my phone with the other. Motherhood had definitely improved my multitasking skills.

Carla had texted back.

Took them home and laundered them. Put them on a counter in the diner's kitchen. Later, they were gone. I assumed Jess had given them to you.

Thanks, I typed into the phone, then hesitated. Should I say something to try to patch things up? I sighed. Not the best thing to attempt via texting.

I put Noelle in her little play yard and sat down on the study's loveseat to think. So, Jess could've put on the clothes and spray painted the bakery wall. But why would she do that after Caleb was dead? Maybe she'd assumed Leroy would still be a competitor. Was the vandalism before or after Leroy had told her he was taking the offending items off of his menu? I couldn't remember.

If Jess was willing to spray paint an obnoxious message on the bakery's wall, did that mean she was capable of murder to protect her diner? I shuddered.

But she has an alibi. Unless Johnny's lying, and Carla had imagined the car engine the morning after Christmas.

Carla could be lying to me now. She could've used the clothes to go on a painting spree herself. But again, *why*, when Caleb was already dead? To scare Dee into leaving town, maybe?

Someone else could've seen the clothes and taken them. Jess

left the back door of the diner unlocked during business hours.

My heart felt heavy in my chest. I wanted it to be the latter option, but I knew it was more likely either Jess or Carla.

I shook my head in frustration, then felt a tugging sensation on my leg. I looked down.

Noelle had escaped the play yard again and was clinging to my jeans, trying to use me to climb onto the loveseat.

I gave her a smile, but it felt a little crooked. Picking her up, I sat her on my lap.

"Ma-ma." She patted my cheek, and I realized it was damp. Tears were leaking from my eyes.

CHAPTER ELEVEN

I'd been neglecting my trainee so, while Noelle was nap-ping, Sugar and I spent an hour doing some refresher exercises. The baby monitor sat on the picnic table nearby, volume turned all the way up.

Sugar, like most Labs, was a bright dog, and she had a good memory. She performed flawlessly. I gave her the off-duty signal, then stroked her cream-colored head and velvety ears. "You're such a good girl."

She was wagging her tail so hard, her whole rear end wig-gled, when suddenly she sat and twitched her ears. The signal that someone was behind me.

I jerked around.

"Yes, I am a good girl," Elise said, grinning. She stood on the back deck, only a few feet away, with Rusty at her side. He let out a soft woof of greeting.

"Didn't mean to sneak up on you," she added, "but I was try-ing not to interrupt the training session. I hope you don't mind." She gestured toward the gate beside the house. "There was no answer out front, but your car was there..."

"No problem. We're done now. What brings you to Mayfair again so soon?"

"A more detailed report on that Leroy Jenkins. You'd said he was a baker, right?"

"Yeah."

"Well," she said, "I couldn't find anywhere that he's done any training—no cooking school, no job at a bakery. The closest he's come to anything food related was a job ten years ago as a stock clerk at Publix."

"Which Publix?"

"The one in Belleview."

That was the grocery store where we shopped. "Hmm, I may drive up there and ask them about Leroy." I paused. "But you could've emailed me all that."

Her cheeks pinked, clashing a little with her bright red hair. "Well, yes, but I'm discovering that I like driving around, to places I know are safe, at least."

I smiled, knowing she didn't mean safe as in crime free, but rather places she had been to and had *not* had a panic attack while there. That's how agoraphobia worked. The underlying panic disorder could set off a panic attack at any time, which was then associated in the person's unconscious mind with that location. After that, the location itself would make the person anxious, which could set off another attack, reinforcing the conditioning.

But now that Elise had Rusty, and her panic disorder was fairly well controlled with medication, she would be able to add more "safe" places to the list.

"Oh, Leroy does have some college under his belt," she added. "He was going to community college at the same time he was working at that store. But he only took general education requirements."

"How did you find out what classes he took?" I asked as I led the way inside the house.

She shook her head. "You don't want to know."

"Yeah, you're probably right." I told Sugar to lie down by the door. I'd crate her later. Then I held up the tea kettle.

Elise nodded. "I was looking to see if he'd taken anything there that might be cooking or baking related."

"So," I said, turning the burner on under the kettle, "a guy with no training convinces another guy with some money to open a bakery with him." I carried mugs and tea bags to the breakfast bar. "Maybe he lied to his partner about the training aspect. And when Caleb found out, he threatened to pull out of the deal, so Leroy whacked him over the head."

"Could be." Elise perched on a stool. "I sent you a list of investors and employees who lost money and/or their jobs when Wilkes's businesses folded, but nobody stands out as having suffered sufficiently to merit murder. The employees are all re-employed, and the investors were rich enough, it didn't really do them any great harm."

I shrugged. "No doubt they wrote it off on their taxes."

"Yeah. You want me to dig any deeper on anyone else?"

"Maybe Dee Wilkes, depending on what Will finds out today. He's tracking down her first husband."

You don't like Deee-Deee? Ms. Snark exaggerated Caleb's nickname for his wife.

Not true. I feel bad for her.

But you don't trust her.

I mentally acknowledged the truth of that. But sadly, I didn't trust most of the people in Mayfair right now. Someone killed Caleb Wilkes, and someone wrote that obnoxious message on the bakery wall. And then someone recklessly fired off a gun in town. Maybe the same someone, maybe not.

But one or more someones in this town were up to no good.

⟵——⟶

A trip to Publix to talk to Leroy's former employer and coworkers could be done with Noelle in tow.

So, after tea and a chat with Elise, we said our goodbyes, and I took Sugar to her crate in the training center. I left her gnawing happily on a chew stick.

Noelle was just waking up, having slept longer than normal, perhaps because of all the excitement this morning. Buddy stood in the nursery doorway watching me change her, his head tilted to one side in his classic *what's-up* look.

"Sorry, boy, but you can't go. They don't allow dogs in grocery stores." I could cheat and put his service dog vest on, but his presence might end up being a distraction for the people I wanted to talk to.

It always felt weird though, when I left the house without him.

I put the puppy in his crate in the study, left a note for Will, and Noelle and I set out for Belleview.

At the store, with Noelle in her stroller, I grabbed a little green basket. I put a can of soup and a package of baby wipes in it, then headed for the bakery section in the back of the store.

Pretending to contemplate what to buy, I struck up a conversation with the young woman behind the counter about the virtues of chocolate chip versus oatmeal raisin cookies.

"You know, we have a new bakery opening up in my town," I said. "And the guy who runs it, I think he used to work here, oh, about ten years ago. His name's Leroy Jenkins."

"Before my time," the young woman said.

I'd figured it would be. "I don't suppose there's anyone who was working here that long ago…" I trailed off, still staring at the cookies on display in the glass case.

"The bakery manager. He's been here over ten years."

I raised my head, wearing what I hoped was a mildly curious expression. "Oh…Would he happen to be in today?"

"Yeah, ya wanna talk to him?"

"Yes, please."

She went into the back and came out a minute later with a burly, middle-aged man swathed in a white apron. He wore a rather unnecessary hairnet over his mostly bald scalp.

"I think I'll have a dozen of the oatmeal raisin." They weren't my favorite so it would be easier to resist them, until Will had eaten them up. She began counting them out.

"There's a new bakery opening up in my town," I said to the manager, in a conversational tone, "and the baker is Leroy Jenkins. I believe he used to work here."

The manager gave me a funny look. "Yes, he worked for the store. It's been years now though."

"He learned how to bake from you? I've only sampled his chocolate chip cookies so far, but they're pretty good." *Understatement of the year!*

He shook his head. "No, he didn't work back here. He was

a stock clerk, but he often hung around during his breaks, and even at the end of his shifts. I was about to ask the store manager if he could transfer to my department, but he got into some trouble with the law."

"He was a good baker, even back then?"

"I didn't know, but I was willing to find out. He said he'd done a lot of baking with his grandma and he loved it. Had a bunch of her original recipes."

"Do you remember anything else about him?"

The man tilted his head to one side. "Not really. Seemed like a nice enough kid. Why do you ask?"

I shrugged. "Oh, I'd heard about his scrape with the law—something to do with fraud—and I guess I'm kind of concerned. The woman he's renting his new shop from is a friend of mine. I don't want to see her get ripped off."

He shook his head. "He always seemed honest enough. The story he told was that his brother got him sucked into something, without him even really knowing what was going on."

"Well, that's a relief." I reached over the top of the case to take the bag of cookies the clerk had been patiently holding out to me.

I put the bag in my basket, waved a cheery goodbye to both of them, and turned Noelle's stroller toward the front of the store.

To be thorough, I went to the customer service desk and asked for the store manager. This time my story was closer to the truth. I introduced myself as a private investigator doing background checks on tenants for a landlady.

"Were you the manager ten years ago, when a Leroy Jenkins worked here?"

"Yes and no. I was the grocery manager back then. Got promoted five years ago."

"Good for you." I gave him a big smile. "So I guess he worked directly for you?"

"Yeah. He was a good worker, until he got himself arrested."

"I heard about that. Do you know any details?"

He scratched his cheek. "Not really, other than it was a perjury charge. I think in a fraud case. The kid kept sayin' he didn't know the guy he'd testified for was fakin' his injuries."

"Did you believe him?"

"Had no reason not to. He'd always been reliable, worked hard. Never caught him stealin' or nothin'…Except now I remember he would often run overtime on his breaks, because he was hangin' out back in the bakery."

"Well, thank you for your time. This has been really helpful."

The manager's forehead furrowed. "I hope this woman you're workin' for doesn't refuse to rent to him because he's got a record."

"Oh, she won't. She believes in giving people the benefit of the doubt."

Noelle and I went through the express line with our few things, where I broke down and bought a candy bar—dark chocolate, my kryptonite.

Once in the car, I compromised with myself, breaking off half and wrapping the other half for later.

I fed a few small pieces to Noelle. "Yummm," I said, exaggerating the *m* sound.

"Yummm," she mimicked and giggled.

As I let a chunk of chocolate dissolve on my tongue, I contemplated the interviews I'd just completed. They corroborated what Leroy had said, but then again, these two men only knew his side of the story regarding the fraud case.

But what he'd told the bakery manager about his grandmother and her recipes did explain why he'd believe he could open a bakery and make a go of it.

And his chocolate chip cookies were further evidence that he was right.

I was tempted to stop at Leroy's shop and ask if Caleb had known he had no formal training as a baker.

However, I wasn't about to do that while Noelle was with me. Not after this morning.

CHAPTER TWELVE

Will was home when we got there. I handed over the oatmeal raisin cookies.

He tried one. "Not bad."

"I bought them as part of my cover."

While he sat on the sofa giving Noelle a horsey ride on his knee, I perched on a breakfast bar stool and told him about Elise's new information on Leroy and what I'd found out at Publix.

Then he, in turn, reported on his chat with Dee Wilkes's ex. "He's a piece of work. Loud and obnoxious–"

"Like Caleb. That seems to be her type."

"Yeah, but not as classy."

I snorted. "I wouldn't exactly call Caleb classy."

"He was classier than this guy. He's a dirtbag, literally. Lives in a trailer that's pretty much trashed inside. Looked and smelled like he hadn't showered in a week. Reeked of beer and marijuana."

"I'm having trouble imagining Dee with someone like that. She's a bit fastidious."

"Maybe he's gone downhill since they were together," Will said.

"Or her OCD tendencies are a reaction to having lived with him."

Noelle gurgled and Will grinned at her. "I did some checking," he continued, "before knocking on his door. She was only eighteen when she married him. During the eight years they were together, there were multiple domestic violence calls to their home—a house that they sold when they divorced. He was arrested several of those times, but she always dropped the charges later."

He shook his head. "A common enough pattern in DV cases, unfortunately. This guy freely admitted that he beat her, said it was because she tended to get lippy."

"I guess she eventually got up the nerve to leave."

"Nope. He claims *he* left *her*, because he caught her cheating on him. Even knew the other guy's name—Broderick Anders. I asked Elise to see what she could find on him."

"Is it time to confront Leroy and/or her again?" I asked. "I was thinking earlier that maybe Leroy hid the fact that he had no formal training from Caleb, and when he found out, they had some kind of argument that ended with the smack on the head with that board."

"Yes, but let's wait to see what Elise digs up on this Anders guy. And we can't both go. One of us has to stay here with Noelle."

On cue, the child blew a raspberry, as if to say, *Hey, you two aren't paying enough attention to me!*

We both laughed.

"But it's not safe for either of us to go alone," I said. "Those two are the only ones in town who seem to have any potential motive to kill Caleb."

"That we know of," Will said, standing up and swinging Noelle around in a circle.

She giggled, and I smiled.

"Now that Edna is paying our expenses," he continued, "maybe we should run background checks on all the other tenants. Someone else might have a connection to Caleb."

"Okay," I said. "I'll email Elise with the info from Edna's files on them. But I still want to talk to Leroy and Dee again."

Will perched Noelle on his hip and ran a hand through his hair. "It really would be best if we both went."

"Hey, remember Mom and Clint are coming tomorrow night and staying over for New Year's Eve. How about I call her and see if they can come earlier and babysit?"

Will nodded. "Sounds like a plan."

⊷——⊷

It had been a long, eventful day, and I was exhausted. But still I tossed and turned some before falling asleep.

A gunshot. I jolted upright.

Wait, I was in bed. *Crapola!* I'd been dreaming.

Or had I? Every muscle tense, I lay still, listening.

Not even crickets. Because even in central Florida, most insects are dormant in winter. I had dreamt the crack of a gun being fired.

I rolled over, trying not to disturb Will, who was softly snoring. Plumping my pillow, I willed myself to settle down.

But my mind would not shut up. Why had someone been firing

off a gun in Mayfair's town limits? And what if this was an indicator of where things were going now that Edna was encouraging strangers to move here?

Okay, that was exactly the insular attitude I did *not* want in my adopted town!

But who could it have been? Billy Baker? He'd gone through a rebellious stage a few years back. But he lived in Gainesville now, a student in Santa Fe College's zoology program. And during the breaks in the school year, he stayed with Jess and Carla at the farm, helping with Jess's small herd of buffalo.

What about young Tony, the Bachman's kid? I hadn't seen hide nor hair of him for at least a year. Wait, he would be at least eighteen by now. Maybe he'd gone off to college too. I made a mental note to check on that.

Could it have been one of the Bakers' girls? No, I couldn't imagine Allie or Sarah touching a gun. They'd been involved in that craziness a few years ago at Halloween, but they were maturing into fairly stable young ladies. Allie, almost sixteen now, helped out some at the diner on weekends.

I rolled over again and stared at the darkness around me. Mayfair had been an idyllic oasis when I'd moved here. I'd fallen in love with the town those first couple of months. Everybody was so friendly and accepting, especially Edna and her nephew Dexter, and Sherie next door.

I'd felt at home for the first time since I'd left my parents' house to marry my first husband—a marriage that had ended quickly and disastrously.

I glanced at my alarm clock. One-ten. I had to get some sleep. I had barn duty in the morning.

This was ridiculous. I threw the covers off in frustration.

Will stirred, and guilt joined frustration and anxiety to make my stomach queasy.

I slipped out of bed, grabbed my robe, and padded down the hall to the nursery. I watched Noelle sleep for a few minutes. Normally, the sight of her little chest rising and falling would be enough to calm my nerves, but not tonight.

I went out to the study and began pacing the floor. This certainly wasn't the first time the outside world had intruded into Mayfair, but each time we'd managed to ward off the evil, and assimilate the good folks, like Susanna's husband Truman, into our ranks.

But this time we'd invited new folks, sight unseen, to make Mayfair their home, or rather Edna had. No, I wasn't going to blame her. She had the town's best interests at heart.

Why hadn't she asked *us* to do more thorough background checks on her new tenants? She would've realized that one of them was Carla's ex-husband if she had.

My mind whirling, I sat down at my desk and opened my laptop, intending to play some online solitaire until I got sleepy again.

But I'd forgotten to shut it down at bedtime. My email program was still open, and at the top of the list of messages was one from Elise.

Apparently, she was also having trouble sleeping tonight, only she'd put her insomnia to better use. The top email's subject line read *Broderick Anders preliminary report*.

I clicked on the email. In her cover note, Elise reported that she'd found a life insurance policy on Caleb Wilkes, that had gone into effect a few months ago. The beneficiary was Dee— not surprising, he'd want to take care of his new bride in case something happened to him.

What was a tad mind-boggling was the size of the policy—half a million dollars. How much would those premiums be? Could Wilkes afford them? Maybe he was better off financially than we'd thought.

I emailed back to Elise, asking her to look for any hidden money, maybe offshore accounts.

I had trouble believing Dee was capable of murder, and she'd seemed genuinely shaken by her husband's death. But Will had hammered it into me that a good detective examines all angles and follows all leads.

If nothing else, maybe I could present the young widow with some good news, that she was better off than she thought she was.

I opened the report on Broderick Anders. He turned out to be yet another guy who wasn't on the up and up. Our very efficient Elise had been unable to find any record of his existence before he'd magically appeared a little over two years ago, a grown man.

Dang, how many fraudsters are there in this part of Florida?

I stared at the man's smiling, boyish face. Fair skinned and dark haired, he oozed charm, even in a photograph.

Who are you really, and how did you get involved with Dee? Had it been a short-term fling or something more serious?

And then it hit me. I didn't know the answer to these questions, *yet.* But Will and I would find them.

We might not be able to keep the real world from contaminating Mayfair occasionally, but we could investigate and identify the bad players, and purge them from our town!

Tomorrow, with any luck, we'd find out if Dee and/or Leroy were among the bad players or were good folks worthy of assimilation. Honestly, I was hoping for the latter for both of them, only because I liked them. But I'd been fooled by a smiling face before.

Speaking of which… I glanced again at Anders's photo. "Maybe you're behind it all?" I muttered.

Suddenly tired beyond belief, I trudged back to the bedroom, shrugged out of my robe and collapsed into bed.

CHAPTER THIRTEEN

The alarm went off way too early. I banged it into silence, before it could wake Will. He rustled some and rolled over.

How was it morning already? It felt like I'd just fallen asleep.

I slipped out of bed and into jeans and an old flannel shirt, plus wool socks, then shuffled out to the study. My laptop was still sitting open where I'd abandoned it last night, but the screen was black. It had gone to sleep.

Not bothering with it, I kept moving toward the kitchen and some much needed caffeine.

I wasn't a morning person by nature, but this was the routine that worked for us right now. On my barn days, I got up super early, so I could get those chores done before Noelle woke up. It didn't always work out, and Will would have to get up to tend to her. But most mornings he slept in some, to make up for the late evenings he often spent doing surveillance.

And most mornings I had at least six to seven hours sleep behind me. However, not this morning, thanks to my ruminations in the middle of the night.

But once I had some coffee in me, I realized I felt lighter than I had in days. My gut was telling me we were close to solving Caleb Wilkes's murder.

My metal travel mug filled with even more coffee and two apples in my barn jacket's pockets, I headed for the stable, Buddy in tow. I might be dragging, but the chilly morning air was perking him up. He trotted ahead of me and ducked under the wooden fence.

In the barn, I fed one apple to my black beauty. She made quick work of it, her lips tickling my palm as she scarfed it up. "No time for a ride this morning, unfortunately." I stroked her velvety nose. "Maybe by tomorrow…" I sighed and made myself get to work.

An hour later, sweet feed had been measured into buckets, stalls had been mucked, and the horses turned out to graze. In front of the barn, Niña touched her nose to Buddy's. He let out a soft woof. She nickered, then tossed her head and romped off across the field.

And I actually felt less tired. The physical labor had gotten my blood flowing.

Back at the house, The smell of burnt toast greeted me. Will and Noelle were up.

She sat in her highchair, squares of dry toast in front of her, only slightly charred on one side.

Will greeted me with a quick kiss. "Breakfast will be ready in a couple of minutes."

My stomach gurgled in response. The apple eaten earlier, between stalls, had already worn off.

I put my barn jacket and boots in the training center, washed my hands, and sat at the breakfast bar. "What's the plan for this confrontation?"

"I'm thinking that we both go armed." Will deftly scooped scrambled eggs onto plates.

I stared at him. I didn't even have a gun.

He stood across the counter from me, grinning. "Me with my Glock and you with your secret weapon." He placed my plate in front of me. "Buddy."

I smiled and Will opened his mouth to say more.

But Noelle interrupted, "Bun-bun." Only yesterday, she'd started calling her stuffed bunny that.

"Bun-bun," she demanded a little louder.

We both chuckled. Will set his plate down. "I'll get it."

Meanwhile I dug into my toast and eggs, sharing some of the latter with Noelle.

The eggs were half gone when I realized Will hadn't come back with the bunny, and Noelle was getting fussier by the second.

I handed her half a slice of my toast. It was buttered, which meant that she would be as well by the time she finished it. But it did the job of distracting her.

I went in search of Will.

He stood in the study, staring down at my computer desk.

"What?" I said.

He shook his head, his expression distracted. "Bunny wasn't in her crib so I was searching for it, and I bumped your desk." He turned the laptop around.

The bogus Broderick Anders was looking back at me from the screen.

"This guy," Will said, his tone incredulous, "is the same dude

I was surveilling last week, the one who went for a nighttime jog. Only his name is Bradford Andrews."

⊷⊶

It was after eleven before I heard the rest of Will's plan. Between the puppy and the baby, the morning had dissolved into our usual state of borderline chaos. Mom had arrived a half hour ago, laden with supplies to make her famous chicken soup and cornbread for dinner tonight.

Which meant she would restock our freezer with leftovers. *Yay!* I helped her unpack, making sure everything was out of Noelle's reach.

Meanwhile, Will sat at the breakfast bar, staring at his phone. Elise had sent the report on Broderick Anders to both of us, of course. And Will was still obsessing over the attached photo.

I walked over and put a hand on his shoulder. "What do you think it means?" I said in a low voice.

"It means we have way too many coincidences," he looked up at me, "and you know how I feel about those." He didn't sound at all happy about this new development.

While Will went to fetch his gun from its safe in our bedroom closet, I made sure Mom had everything she needed to watch Noelle. Clint had begged off from coming early and was joining us this evening.

We walked toward the new shops, Buddy on his leash, and Will wearing an untucked flannel shirt, the tail hanging over his gun in its waistband holster.

"So, what's the rest of your plan?" I asked.

"It's more like a loose outline of how things might go,

depending on who's in the bakery. If it's just Dee, you take the lead and I'm your backup, and vice versa, if it's just Leroy."

I nodded. "And if they're both there?"

"We both go in," he said, "and I think we'll start by asking if Caleb knew that Leroy has no training as a baker."

"Except at his grandmother's knee, that is."

"We still don't have the report back on the bike guy," Will said, sounding slightly annoyed.

"We've been throwing requests at Elise fast and furious lately," I pointed out.

"True. What's your take on him?"

I shrugged. "Potheads are usually fairly mellow, but he got a bit belligerent when I pointed out that recreational marijuana use is still illegal in Florida."

"Maybe we'll pay Gates a visit as well, after we talk to whoever's at the bakery. Paranoia can be a long-term effect of marijuana, so if he's been smoking the stuff all his life..." He trailed off, as we stepped up onto the boardwalk.

I squinted at the bakery's plate-glass window. "Don't see either one of them in there."

"I doubt they're taking the day off, not when they're supposed to open in two days." Will tried the door. It was locked.

"Leroy was baking things yesterday," I said, "getting a feel for his new oven. Let's check around back, see if he's in the kitchen."

The back door was indeed sitting open, letting the heat out. Will eased his head around the doorjamb. "Leroy," he whispered. "He's by himself."

I nodded and he went inside.

I stepped up onto the edge of the wooden stoop, where I could peek in without being seen. Buddy automatically took up the cover position, facing behind me.

"Hey, Leroy." Will's voice. "How's it going?"

"Good," Leroy said. "Everything's ready to go for our opening, except I'm still adjusting the baking times for some of my recipes. This oven runs hot. Hey, you want to take home a cherry pie? If it turns out right this time, that is."

"Sure. My in-laws are here for the weekend. Say, where did you learn to bake anyway?"

A pause, the creak of an oven door opening, then clanking closed. "Needs a few more minutes. Mostly I learned from my grandmother. She lived with us for a while, when I was growing up."

"No formal training?"

Silence. I peeked around the edge of the doorjamb. In jeans and a light blue tee shirt, Leroy was at a worktable rolling out dough. "Not really," he finally answered. "I was gonna go to culinary school, but…life got in the way."

"Uh-huh, like a sentence for fraud."

Leroy looked up at Will. "Yeah. And I already told your wife all about that."

"Right, you were innocent, didn't know what was going on." Will's voice had a disbelieving edge.

Leroy frowned at him, his lips a tight line. "I didn't."

"How long have you known Dee and Caleb Wilkes?" Will changed tacks, I assumed to ease the tension so Leroy wouldn't clam up.

"Caleb about six months. I've known Dee longer."

Interesting. I peeked around the jamb again. Leroy was rolling out more dough. A pie pan with a bottom layer and apple filling sat next to him.

"How much longer?" Will asked.

Leroy shrugged, his attention on the strips of dough he was cutting to make a lattice top on the pie. "About two years, I guess."

"Did they know you didn't have any formal training?" Will asked.

Leroy's head jerked up. "Yes. Caleb didn't care, once he tasted my baked goods." There was a touch of pride in his voice.

"Well, I guess that is the ultimate criteria," Will said with a chuckle. "Your cookies sure are good."

Leroy glanced up, gave him a small smile, and went back to his task.

I was fascinated by how Will alternated between being a little confrontational and then easing off.

"Well, if you've known Dee that long, I guess you know this guy too." Will held up his phone with her ex-boyfriend's photo on it.

Leroy gasped. "Where'd you get a picture of my brother?"

Wait, what? Broderick Anders was Leroy's brother? But Anders was *white*.

Half-brothers, Ms. Snark reminded me, just as Buddy's tail thumped against the wooden stoop.

I glanced down. His ears were twitching. Someone was behind me.

Two more soft sounds—that I would've missed without Buddy's signal. The snick of a safety being disengaged and the click of a revolver being cocked.

An icy shiver ran down my spine.

CHAPTER FOURTEEN

I whirled around. Dee Wilkes stood a few feet away.

Her face—which had been soft and sweet-looking most of the times I'd seen her before—was now pinched, her blue eyes icy. "It may be small," she nodded at the snub-nose pistol in her hand, "but it'll put a good-sized hole in you." She gestured toward the door. "Now, go on in."

Buddy growled.

"And shut your dog up," she added. "I've heard about your tricks. If you tell him to grab me, I'll shoot him first and then you, and then that nosy husband of yours. Now get inside!"

I went through the doorway, my hands partway up. "Who told you about Buddy's tricks, as you call them."

"That woman at the motel, our landlady's niece. It wasn't hard to pump her for information about you and some others in town."

Dear, sweet Susanna. She was such an innocent, and she

liked to talk.

Will and Leroy had turned toward us, Leroy staring and Will reaching behind his back.

"Don't!" Dee yelled. She grabbed my arm, pulled me in tight next to her. "You try anything and I shoot your wife. Leroy, get his gun."

"What are you doing, Dee?" Leroy's voice was desperate. "I don't want to go back to prison."

"And you won't. Now get his gun."

Hesitantly, Leroy walked to Will and pulled the Glock from his waistband.

"Put it over there on that side table," she said.

He moved slowly in that direction, holding the gun away from himself like it might bite him.

"Dee was dating your brother, huh," Will said to him, in a conversational tone. He sounded calm, but I suspected he was far from that state.

"How'd she end up with Caleb?" he asked.

"I introduced them." Leroy put Will's gun on the smaller table, but he didn't move back toward us. "Last summer, Caleb and I were at a bar making plans for the bakery, when Rick walked in with this one on his arm."

"You lied about losing contact with him then," I said.

Leroy shrugged. "I tried to avoid him."

Dee laughed. "You thought we just happened to run into you, but it was all planned. Rick heard you were going into business with some rich guy, and we figured he'd make a good mark." She sneered. "I pretended I was madly in love with the old fool, and he lapped it up."

"And I suppose Rick acting all jealous was exactly

that—acting." Leroy's voice had some anger in it now.

Dee ignored him, her eyes on Will and me.

"You married Caleb for his money," I said, following the adage of keep them talking. "But he wasn't the great businessman he pretended to be. He wasn't nearly as wealthy as you'd thought."

"No, and he made me sign a prenuptial agreement. I wouldn't get anything if we divorced, only if he died."

"So you killed him," Will said.

"Now I'll have to wait for his will to go through probate," Dee said, "but there's a nice fat insurance policy in the meantime."

She tilted her head toward Leroy. "And he can run his bakery for now, build it up so it's worth something. I've identified a couple of easy marks here in town. Once I've gotten their money, we'll sell the business and get out of here."

Leroy scowled at her. "I'm not selling my bakery!"

Dee shifted slightly toward him.

Will's body tensed.

He's waiting for an opening. My stomach roiled. If he rushed her, he might get himself shot.

Then Dee's words sank in. And my fear for Will and myself morphed into a greater horror. If we didn't stop this woman, who knew what havoc she'd wreak on our town.

"You'll do as you're told," Dee was saying to Leroy, "if you truly don't want to go to prison again. Remember, you helped me move the body."

"You knew she'd killed him?" I blurted out.

"I thought it was self-defense," Leroy said, his voice moving toward frantic. "She said he hit her, and she grabbed the board to defend herself, that it was an unlucky blow." He turned anguished eyes toward me. "I believed her. Caleb had a history of hitting women. And I panicked. With him dead, if Dee went to jail…I was afraid I'd lose the bakery."

I clenched my fists, anger filling my chest. "And you had no trouble letting Jess take the blame. You both would've let her go to prison, if it weren't for us."

"Yeah," Dee sneered again, "if it weren't for your meddling–"

"I would've stepped up," Leroy interrupted her, "if it looked like Jess was going to be convicted."

Dee ignored him again, raised her gun arm. "I'm gonna enjoy shooting the two of you."

"You're not shooting anybody." Leroy grabbed up Will's pistol and aimed it at Dee, but his hands shook.

Dee moved her gun to halfway between Will and Leroy. "Put that down, you fool."

"No, you drop *your* gun!" Leroy screeched.

Dee turned farther toward him.

"Buddy, knees!" I prayed he remembered the command. We hadn't practiced it recently, and I'd never used it in real life before.

But he remembered. He slammed into the woman's knees at the same moment Will dove toward her. The crack of a gunshot and they all went down in a heap.

My already hammering heart jumped into my throat. *Please God, let them be okay.*

The .32 had skittered across the floor.

"Get gun!" That command I *had* used before, all too often.

Buddy disentangled himself, scrambled to his feet and ran for the weapon. Will seemed unhurt as well, as he struggled with a flailing Dee.

I breathed a quick sigh of relief. The shot had gone astray.

Dee landed an elbow in Will's rib cage. He let out an "Oof," but continued to hold onto her. She cursed a blue streak.

"Stop fighting him, Dee," Leroy yelled, "or I'll shoot."

I jerked around. He was shaking even worse, still holding the Glock, pointed toward Will and Dee.

My stomach heaved. "No!" I screamed. "Put the gun down. Will's got her."

Leroy turned slightly toward me, a dazed look on his face. He dropped his arms, letting the gun slide to the floor.

Then his eyes rolled back in his head, and he went down, a red splotch expanding slowly on the side of his tee shirt.

EPILOGUE

New Year's Eve was an evening of many surprises, beginning with the fact that my husband owned a tuxedo. How did I not know that?

"I bought it when I thought I'd be running for re-election for sheriff in Collins County," he said, as I straightened his bow tie.

"So you wore it exactly once before." I chuckled. "When you attended that fundraiser…"

He chuckled back. "The one I cut out of early to talk to you."

I turned so he could zip up my dress. It was midnight blue, with a tight bodice and a flared, knee-length skirt that disguised my ample hips.

Will did the honors, then kissed my neck. A thrill ran through me.

"You're gorgeous," he murmured.

"Why, thank you, kind sir," I said over my shoulder.

A knock on our bedroom door. "Someone wants to say good-night." Elise's voice.

I opened the door and accepted the child who was thrust into my arms.

Noelle planted a slobbery kiss on my cheek. "Ma-ma."

I held her tight, sucking in the smell of freshly bathed baby, which only increased the intense pressure in my chest. I loved this little being more than life itself. "Happy New Year, sweetie," I whispered in her ear.

She blew a raspberry, and Elise moved her on to say good-night to her father.

I stepped past them and walked out through the study and into the living room. And encountered the second surprise of the night.

My mother's husband also was wearing a tux and wearing it well, despite his big frame. He grinned at me. "Happy New Year!"

I was grinning back until I spotted Mom behind Clint, in a tight black dress covered with sequins. It was long-sleeved and knee-length, but still…super sexy?

I felt a tiny bit queasy. One does not like to think of one's mom as sexy.

"Wow!" I couldn't come up with anything else to say.

Mom gave me a preening smile, and I heard the rustle of the old biddies from my father's church turning over in their graves.

Elise came into the room, Noelle on one hip. "Go on, all of you! I've got things under control, and you're only three blocks away."

Will stepped up and draped a light blue silk stole over my shoulders. "Let's go."

As we walked to the diner in the slight evening chill, he filled us in on the status of the case. The assistant state's attorney's office had given Will a courtesy call since he'd taken down the killer.

"What, you didn't give Buddy credit for helping?" My tone was mock offended.

"I did." Will smiled down at me. "Turns out Leroy's wound wasn't too bad. He's already been released from the hospital, and he's getting probation in exchange for his cooperation in making a case against Dee Wilkes."

"Good," I said. "I couldn't help liking him, even if he was one of our main suspects."

"And I'm glad his cookies will be permanently available just a short walk from home."

"Ugh." I patted one hip. "Not sure that's a good or a bad thing."

"You look beautiful," Mom said from behind me.

"And so do you," I said. Then Ms. Snark snuck past my defenses and added, "Quite sexy!"

Heat rose in my cheeks. *Behave!* I told her internally.

You're no fun.

I glanced over my shoulder. In the yellowish glow of the streetlight above us, I could see Mom was also blushing, but smiling too. And Clint was grinning from ear to ear—probably working hard not to bust out laughing.

And my heart expanded at the sight. I was so glad Mom had this man in her life! He made her happy, and he was truly a nice guy.

"Indeed," Will was saying, "the case against Dee is strong enough that the ASA got her to confess, which means we won't have to testify."

I blew out a relieved sigh. "Thank heavens! Did she do the graffiti and the gunshots as well?"

"She did. She was trying to keep things stirred up, and to shift attention away from herself as a suspect."

"But why the random shots?" I asked.

Will looked down at me. "Do you really want to know?"

"Yes." At least, I thought I did.

"She saw you with Noelle in the stroller and wanted to scare you, thinking it might get you to stop poking around."

Mom gasped behind us.

Anger flared in my chest. "That b–" I caught myself as a cuss word was about to escape, and in front of my mother!

Clint chuckled. "I was thinking the same word."

"You behave," Mom said, but with a hint of laughter in her own voice.

I gently jabbed Will with my elbow. "And stop calling it 'poking around.' I was legitimately investigating for a client."

Will gave me a teasing grin, then said, "I also got a call from the Levy County sheriff's office."

"Oh?"

"They arrested Broderick Anders, aka Bradford Andrews, and guess what they found?" We had reached the corner of Main Street and Mayfair Avenue.

"What?" We stepped off the curb and crossed the street.

"A burner phone," Will said, "with the same number as the guy who was calling and claiming I hit him with my truck."

I stopped short in front of the diner. Mom almost ran into me. "Really?" I exclaimed.

He nodded. "Really."

"Wow, now *that* is a coincidence."

"Not so much," Will said. "He's a con man through and through. He figured the insurance company was about to pay up for his bogus injuries from that fender bender, so it was time to set up his next mark. Oh, and his real name is Richard Anderson. He and Leroy share the same mother.”

“Meanwhile, his girlfriend was running her own con on Caleb Wilkes.” The proverbial lightbulb went off in my head. “It was only one couple. We didn’t have multiple con artists, vandals and murderers wreaking havoc. It was just *two* people.” Muscles that had been tense for almost a week finally relaxed.

Clint’s stomach growled loudly, reminding us that we were at our destination.

He stepped forward and grabbed the handle of the diner’s door. “Ladies first.” Mom went ahead of me.

I stepped into the diner and gasped, my mouth falling open. The room was lit by a thousand tiny lights strung across the ceiling. Candles flickered on the tables, which were set with fine china and silverware, on top of white linen tablecloths.

Jess drifted across the fairyland room, in a white, off-the-shoulder evening gown. Johnny Redmond trailed behind, looking a little self-conscious in a rented tux.

I opened my mouth. “Jess, I’m so sor–”

She pulled me into a hug before I could finish the sentence. “I’m the one who’s sorry. I should’ve trusted you.”

She broke the hug and held me at arm’s length. “Thank you for saving my keister, again!”

I assumed she was referring to when Dan, her first fiancé, was killed.

“And you look marvelous,” she added.

“Ditto, on both counts,” Johnny said, grinning from ear to ear.

I smiled as Carla swept into our little group, wearing a green silk dress with a knee-length, flared skirt similar to mine. “There you are," she said to me, her expression neutral.

My heart stuttered for a second. *Is she still mad at me?*

But she seemed relaxed. Russ Fortham stepped up beside her. Bear, his Chow-Husky service dog dropped into the cover position next to him.

I was surprised to see Russ was wearing his Air Force dress uniform.

"I'm still in the reserves," he said.

I felt my cheeks flush, that he'd caught me staring at his uniform. I greeted him awkwardly, not used to rubbing elbows with my former veteran clients socially.

He grinned at me and apparently read my expression accurately again. "I'm gonna be around a lot, Marcia, so get used to it." He pulled up Carla's hand, now linked with his own, to expose a sparkling sapphire ring. "We're pre-engaged."

I blew out air as warmth spread through my chest. "Congratulations!"

Carla frowned at him. "I thought we weren't going to make a big deal about it."

"Sorry, sweetheart," he said, not looking the least bit sorry. He turned to Will. "This is really weird. I thought it was the guy who was supposed to be afraid of commitment."

Will laughed. "Not in this day and age." He pointed his thumb at me. "Took me two years to wear her down."

At that, Carla grinned at me.

And I relaxed again. She too had forgiven me for sticking my nose in her business.

Russ gave Bear the release signal, so I could scratch his ears and say hi. Carla and I had worked together to train the dog, who did indeed remind one of a big teddy bear.

Then Will led me across the room to the large round table in the middle of the floor. Place-setting cards indicated where we were supposed to sit. The two cards next to me read *Edna* and *Dexter*, and *Claire* and *Clint* were on the other side of Will. There were two other place settings across the table. But those cards were facing away from me.

We sat and I scanned the room—recognizing some of the new shop owners, but other faces were strangers to me.

Who are these people?

Nobody you can't handle, Ms. Snark said inside my head.

Wait, are you being…supportive?

I expected a flip response, such as, *In your dreams.* But the internal silence stretched out.

Thanks! I said internally.

You're welcome.

Edna came over and took her seat, her great-nephew beside her. He was a brick or two short of a load, thanks to the battering Susanna had endured while pregnant with him, at the hands of her now long-deceased first husband.

But Dexter was the sweetest guy ever. He was not wearing a tux, but he'd cleaned up good, in a button-down shirt and tie, and black jeans.

"Hey, Dex," I said, "you look great."

He blushed and gave me an *aw-shucks* grin.

Edna wore a satiny red blouse, which I suspected she'd made herself—sewing being one of her main hobbies these days. The blouse hung loose over black stretch pants. And in honor of the occasion, her black flip-flops were covered in sequins.

Mom and Clint arrived at the table. They were both smiling, probably over some joke one of them had just told.

Ding, ding, ding. A sixtyish man, also in a dress shirt and tie, was tapping his empty champagne glass. I spotted the gray pony-tail and realized it was Barry Gates, the aging hippie with the bike rental shop. He cleaned up pretty good too.

He cleared his throat. "On behalf of the other new shop owners, I'd like to propose a toast."

Lisa and the new waitress were circulating the room, filling the flutes with champagne. Lisa gave the guy a frantic look, and the two of them stepped up their pace.

They had no need to worry, though. He turned out to be long-winded.

Starting to get bored, I tuned him out and scanned the crowd. I spotted Sherie, and Sybil was with her. I caught the latter's eye and discreetly waved. She grinned and waved back, not nearly as discreetly.

Susanna and her husband, Truman were at the same table. Susanna also gave me a small wave. Was that a smirk on her face?

The Bakers were across the room, their two eldest with them. Allie spotted me, grinned, then leaned over to whisper to her parents. The rest of the family turned, smiled and nodded. They seemed a bit off to me, a little too cheerful perhaps, even for New Year's Eve.

"...so despite all that, the murder and such," Barry was saying, "thank you for welcoming all of us to your beautiful town."

I zoned out again, and missed a few words.

"...ads and news releases, tomorrow should be a smashing success." A round of applause greeted this pronouncement.

Wait, what? Ads and news releases...what have you done, Edna?

"So, without further ado," the man raised his champagne flute, "to Edna Mayfair *and* to a successful New Year!"

Glasses clinked around the room.

Will and I tapped ours together, and I took a sip. The champagne was delicious, but I dared not drink too much of it on an empty stomach.

On cue, Lisa and the other young woman appeared, carrying trays laden with soup bowls. Lisa set one in front of each of us at our table, except for Edna.

I leaned toward my octogenarian friend. "I thought you loved Jess's seafood bisque."

She gave me an enigmatic half smile.

I was distracted by a rustling noise. I looked up and into my best friend's sparkling eyes, as she settled across the table from me. Becky wore a pink dress that accentuated her curvy body. Dark curls framed her heart-shaped face.

I suppressed the urge to squeal and run around the table to hug her. I settled for exchanging a grin.

Her husband, Andy sat down next to her, looking quite handsome in a white tux that contrasted nicely with his light tan skin and close-cropped dark hair. He too was grinning.

We sure are doing a lot of that tonight.

Clink, clink. Edna had risen to her feet and was tapping her spoon against her glass. "May I have your attention, please. By all means, continue to enjoy Jess's excellent soup, but I want to acknowledge the stars of *this* year, before we move on to the next one."

She turned toward me and Will. "I want to officially thank Will and Marcia for investigatin' and clearin' Jess's name. You two…well, Lady Justice may be blind, but you two sure have a way of spellin' things out to her in Braille."

Ripples of laughter around the room.

"So it is my pleasure…," Edna said, as Dexter rose, an ear-splitting grin on his face. They walked around behind Will and me. "…to bestow upon the two of you the first ever Mayfair Medals of Honor." They draped gold medals, suspended from blue ribbons, around our necks.

Gales of laughter from Ms. Snark within. My mouth twitched as I struggled to rein her in.

"As always, you two went above and beyond," Edna was saying, her voice choked up some, "to protect our community, and we are so lucky to have you as part of our Mayfair family."

A lump formed in my own throat.

Edna raised her champagne flute. "To Marcia and Will, may their PI agency thrive so they can continue to protect good people from the evil in the world."

More clinking of glasses. "Hear, hear," echoed around the room.

Ha, no pressure! Ms. Snark chortled inside.

You had *to have the last word, didn't you?*

She snickered.

◆————◆

AUTHOR'S NOTES

If you enjoyed this book, please take a moment to leave a short review on the ebook retailer of your choice. Reviews help with sales and sales keep the stories coming. You can readily find the links to these retailers at https://misteriopress.com/bookstore/.

Sadly, this is the last installment in this thirteen-story series (more on this in a moment). The story just prior to this one is *To Bark or Not to Bark*. (For all my stories, please see the list of series at the front of this book.)

This book was proofread by multiple sets of eyes, but proofreaders are human. If you noticed any errors, please email me at kass@kassandralamb.com so I can have them corrected.

Heck, email me anyway. I love hearing from readers!

And you may want to sign up for my newsletter at https://kassandralamb.com to get a heads up about new releases, plus special offers and bonuses for subscribers. You will also receive a free novelette, *The Tell-Tale Bark*, the prequel to this series, AND a free novella, *Sweet Sanctuary*, the prequel to my traditional mystery series, the Kate Huntington Mysteries.

Also, *misterio press* now has a readers' group on Facebook (https://www.facebook.com/groups/misteriopressmysteries/) where we chat with readers and offer giveaways and other goodies. Please stop by and check it out!

Bear with me as I spread some gratitude around, before I go into why it is time to end this series. There are several people who played key roles in making these stories a reality. First, there was and is my friend Angi, whose encouragement from the beginning kept me writing when I was sure I would never produce anything worthy of others' time to read it. And she has also acted as one of my consultants on service dog training. Then there is my friend and cofounder of *misterio press*, Shannon Esposito—it's been quite a journey, hasn't it, Shan? And all the other lovely ladies at misterio are so supportive of me and each other. I am so, so lucky to have found all of you!

Special appreciation is due to Shannon, Kirsten Weiss, Liz Boeger and Sasscer Hill for their helpful critiques and proofreading of this particular story. And also to Marilyn Hiliau, one of my long-term loyal readers, who has also consulted on service-dog training issues.

Indeed, a heartfelt thank you goes out to all my long-term readers, who started with me when Kate Huntington was solving her first few crimes and have stuck with me all this time since. You all are the greatest!!

Another person who has made a huge impact on my writing and my success is my editor, Marcy Kennedy. I can't say enough about what an amazing teacher she is!! I have learned so much from her and continue to depend on her to catch my plot holes and make sure my characters don't wander off the path too far.

And last but not least, my patient husband. It took him awhile to realize I was serious about this writing thing…after all, wasn't I supposed to be retired? But he's been so supportive, by hawking my books to anyone who will listen (including the nurse pushing his gurney down a hospital hallway after an operation), by proofreading, and by putting up with my weird writerly ways (like staying up until 3 a.m. revising a manuscript).

And I'm far from done! I have a new series started. But first, why am I ending this one?

It is always a bittersweet experience for a writer to end a series. You are saying goodbye to dear friends, knowing you will never see nor speak to them again—not even an email or a text.

But there comes a point when ending the series seems like the right thing to do, for several reasons.

One, you run out of story ideas that are well suited for that particular set of characters and that setting. In the Kate series, I thought this had happened with *Anxiety Attack*, and had planned for it to be the last book. Then the idea for *Police Protection* came to me, so I wrote it. I'm very glad I did, because that story did a better job of bringing closure to Kate around her first husband's death. And I think it's one of the best stories in the series.

But this time, I was more methodical about planning the end of the series. I knew going into Book 9 it would be the last full-length novel that included a military veteran as a central character. And I already had plans for this last holiday novella, *Auld Lang Mayfair*, so I could tie up loose ends of what was happening in Marcia's little town.

The other major reason for ending a series is when the protagonist has completed what writers call their "character arc."

Like real people, main characters start out with flaws, issues, maybe even neuroses, that hark back to their pasts. Ideally, as they encounter the challenges of each book in a series, they should move slowly, although sometimes haltingly, towards overcoming those issues.

I feel that Marcia has done this, for the most part. She started out a bit immature, a little impulsive, and more than a tad gun-shy of anything resembling commitment in a relationship, thanks to

her first disastrous marriage. And one issue went back even farther than that. She'd always struggled with the desire to be "normal," while secretly she reveled a bit in being different.

If not, then why didn't she just tell her classmates growing up
to call her Marsha? Why did she correct people when they mis-
pronounced her name?

Because secretly she liked it; it made her more unique. This
is one of the many things she's figured out about herself over the
course of the years since she moved to Florida, to take on the not
so "normal" job of service dog trainer.

I hoped you've enjoyed riding along on her journey as much
as I have.

But why not stay with her for a while longer, you might ask.

Because her "arc" has naturally led her to become a private
detective. It's the right outcome for her, but it's not what this series
is about. This series is about a service dog trainer and amateur
sleuth, so it's time for me to move on, wishing her and her loved
ones all the best!

The third and lesser of the reasons for ending a series is that I
love a challenge. Thus the shifts in sub-genre, from a traditional,
amateur sleuth series to a cozy format (small town, quirky characters), and now to police procedurals.

Changing gears to something new tends to inspire and re-ener-
gize me. Maybe I'll come back and write some private detective
stories about Marcia and Will at some point in the future.

But for now, I am loving the challenge of writing police procedurals, and developing the character of Chief of Police Judith
Anderson (from the Kate Huntington series, so you see, there is
hope I will recycle other characters as well).

So please stay with me as I move ahead with this new series.

I promise to do my best to continue to entertain!

To lure you along, here's an excerpt from Book 2 in the C.o.P. on the Scene Mysteries.

Excerpt from *Fatal Escape, A C.o.P. on the Scene Mystery*:

CHAPTER ONE

As usual, I was awake before the sun. But the grim reaper had also risen early today.

I roust myself out of bed predawn so I can get in some exercise, before that day's quota of defecation hits the ventilation system.

Not happening this morning, though. I was only on my ninth push-up when I got the call. Shoving myself up off the floor, I grabbed my police-issue cell phone. "Chief Anderson," I barked.

"Good morning, Chief," an undaunted Bradley replied. "We've got a scene on the Sofki Bridge that I thought you'd wanna see before the body's transported."

"Homicide?" I stepped into the bathroom, got the shower running.

"Not sure. Looks like a suicide on first blush. Of course, the medical examiner will make the final call, but…"

"…something looks suspicious."

"Yeah."

I could've pushed for more info, but that would've only slowed me down. Sergeant Bradley, my second in command, would not be calling without good reason.

"Be there in twenty minutes." Ten to shower and dress, ten to get to the scene. Ours was not a big city and there would be little traffic on a Sunday morning.

Eight minutes later, I had donned my least favorite black pantsuit—crime scenes can be hard on one's clothes—and I was stuffing badge and phone into the jacket pockets. My Glock slid smoothly into its middle-of-the-back holster. I glanced in the mirror over my dresser.

Dark hair, still damp, stuck out in places. No time for a comb, I used my fingers to smooth it down into what my mother had called a pixie cut.

I growled softly under my breath. *I'm no damn pixie, that's for sure.* But the short hairstyle was easy to maintain.

The Sofki Bridge, named after the tributary of the St. John's River that it spans, is the smaller of two bridges linking our city of Starling to Jacksonville, where at least half of our residents work. It's only one lane in each direction, with a center lane that reverses direction depending on the time of day.

Despite being Sunday, some cars were already lining up on the Starling end. I pulled off on the shoulder and called Bradley as I hoofed it the rest of the way to the crime scene. "I'm here. What have we got?"

"Two locations," he said. "Abandoned car up here on the bridge and a body pulled out of the river that's on the pier below."

I spotted an ambulance ahead, with two paramedics, looking bored, beside it. Beyond was yellow crime scene tape, stretched between two trees on either side of a dirt path leading down to the pier.

"Who's lead?"

"Cruthers," Bradley said, "but I assigned Patterson to help out, until we know what we've got."

"Be up top in a minute." Disconnecting, I nodded to the paramedics and trotted toward the crime scene tape on the dirt path. I should've grabbed my sneakers instead of the low-heeled pumps I usually wear to the office.

Two men stood silhouetted by the streetlights along the pier, their backs to me. Beyond them, a woman's bare legs stretched across the wooden planks, one shoe missing.

A uniformed officer, dripping wet, sat nearby on the side of the pier. He shivered under a shiny silver blanket draped around his shoulders, no doubt provided by the paramedics.

"You called her?" one of the standing men said to the other.

"Nah, Bradley did," the other answered.

The dripping officer turned his head. His eyes went wide when he saw me.

"Better him waking her up than me," the second man continued. "He's got his nose so far up her butt…" He trailed off when the uniform cleared his throat.

The man turned, the lights overhead revealing the face of Detective Patterson. He faked a smile. "Good morning, Chief."

"Good morning." Not sure what to do about the disrespectful comment, I opted to pretend I hadn't heard it, for now. "I'm going up top to check in."

The other man had also turned. He was in uniform, my newest sergeant, Armstrong, recently promoted to watch commander. His expression was grim.

"In the meantime," I said, "how about getting some more tape up around this part of the scene." I glanced meaningfully up to the road above, where some folks were getting out of their cars, trying to see what was going on.

Armstrong's cheeks flushed, but Patterson's bogus smile hung on. "Sure thing, Chief."

"Come with me," I said to the seated officer. He jumped up and followed me.

I glanced at his name tag. *Dulles. Shouldn't be hard to remember, like the airport in Washington, D.C.*

"You were first on the scene, Officer Dulles?"

"Yes, Chief." His teeth chattered. "It was called in as an abandoned vehicle. But when I ran my flashlight beam over the river, I spotted a clump of clothes, caught in the grasses on this side, downstream some. I came down here to the pier to get a better look." He jerked his head toward the river. "Turned out to be her."

"So you went in after her?"

"Yes, ma'am, in case she was still alive." He shook his head mournfully.

"Describe her." I'd get a better look at the body eventually, once the ME's people arrived, but I wanted to hear his impressions.

"Short, petite, except she's curvy." He gestured with his hands to indicate a voluptuous figure. Then grabbed for the edges of the blanket as it attempted to slither off his shoulders.

"Long black hair. Light tan skin. I think she's...uh, was Hispanic. Tight red dress, short. But her shoes are black sneakers—or should I say, shoe. She's missing one."

We'd reached the official entrance to the crime scene, where another uniform was keeping the crime scene entry log. He noted my entry and tilted his head to one side. "The detectives are over by the car, Chief."

I nodded my thanks and headed that way, Dulles dripping along beside me. "Did you call for the detectives?"

"Yes, ma'am. Couple of things felt off. One, I couldn't find any purse or wallet in the car."

"You searched the car?" My voice rose a bit.

"No, ma'am," he said quickly, his face anxious. "Only with my eyes. I didn't touch anything. But the driver's door was hanging open, the overhead light on, and the contents of the glove box were dumped out on the passenger seat and floor. No sign of a purse or wallet, that I could see."

"She might've taken it with her into the river." Although that would not be typical suicidal behavior. You don't need your possessions if you plan to be dead, and usually the suicide wants people to know who they are.

"Well, then there was…" We'd reached the front fender of the car. He gestured toward the guard rail along the side of the bridge. "On the railing, something's smeared there. I, uh, think it's blood."

"Good call." To Bradley and Cruthers who were now approaching us, I said, "You need this officer right now?"

They both shook their heads.

"Go home and change your uniform, Dulles."

Sergeant Armstrong had walked up.

"Is that okay with you?" I asked him. Technically, the uniforms were his province.

"No problem. Uh, Chief, could I speak to you for a moment?"

"Does it relate to this case?"

"No."

"Then later, my office in an hour." My tone was more terse than I'd intended. I decided I was okay with that.

"Got it." Armstrong turned away.

"Did you all know the corpse is missing a shoe?" I asked.

Cruthers nodded his shaggy dark head. He was a big guy,

always reminded me of a bear. "It probably came off in the water."

"Maybe, but she's wearing a sneaker, so less likely to have come off on its own. And it's out of sync with the rest of her attire."

Cruthers nodded again and beckoned to a couple of uniforms nearby. "Look for a sneaker." He glanced my way.

"Black."

"But don't touch anything inside the car until the CS team gets here," Cruthers was saying as he walked away with them.

Barnes suddenly appeared at my elbow. I jumped a little.

"Sorry," my short but sturdy assistant said. Even at this hour, she was meticulously turned out, in a well-pressed uniform, her dark hair up in a sleek bun. "I didn't mean to sneak up on you, Chief."

"How'd you know I was here?" I asked.

She grinned. "Heard the calls for an ambulance and detectives on the radio. Where else would you be?"

"Can you help with the search, we're looking for–"

"A black woman's sneaker. I heard." Barnes jogged off to join the other uniforms.

"CS guys are on their way with a warrant," Bradley said, "to take the car back to our lot." He skimmed slightly-too-long brown hair out of his blue eyes. Like Barnes—his sister—he was impeccably dressed, only his "uniform" was a navy business suit.

I scanned the scene. More looky-loos were getting out of their cars. "We need to get one lane open as soon as possible." I could imagine the mayor yelling about inconveniencing the citizens, as if that took precedence over investigating a woman's death.

"Yeah." Bradley said, a grimace on his handsome face. "Otherwise, we're gonna need the auxiliary people for crowd control."

"Actually, that's not a bad idea. Call them in."

Bradley grimaced again. He apparently shared the opinion of quite a few officers regarding the recently formed auxiliary group—that the "wannabe cops" were a hazard as often as they were a help. But Mr. Mayor was constantly searching for ways to save money. The word *volunteer* was a favorite of his. And the auxiliary folks were able to lighten the load at times like these.

"We don't want to open the bridge though," Bradley was saying, "until the CS guys see those." He pointed to the road in front of the car.

The sun was still below the horizon but the predawn sky revealed black streaks on an angle in front of the abandoned car.

"Looks like someone may have veered in front of her and then slammed on their brakes," Bradley said. "There are skid marks behind her car as well. Two sets. One belongs to the commuter who almost rammed into the car's back end. He called 911."

I nodded.

"Have you seen the body yet?" he asked.

"Not up close."

Bradley made an after-you gesture. We walked to the end of the bridge, ignoring the questions some drivers were throwing our way.

The ME's van was now parked behind my car. Bradley and I picked up speed, jogging down the dirt path.

We got to the pier just in time to watch the assistant ME turn the body over.

There was a bloody gash on the back of the dead woman's head.

ABOUT THE AUTHOR

Kassandra Lamb has never been able to decide which she loves more, psychology or writing. In college, she realized that writers need a day job in order to eat, so she studied psychology. After a career as a psychotherapist and college professor, she is now retired and can pursue her passion for writing.

She spends most of her time in an alternate universe with her characters. The portal to that universe, aka her computer, is located in Florida, where her husband and dog catch occasional glimpses of her.

Kass has completed ten full-length novels in the Kate Huntington Mystery series (set in her native Maryland, about a psychotherapist/amateur sleuth), plus four Kate on Vacation novellas (with the same characters). She is also the author of the Marcia Banks and Buddy cozy mystery series, about a service dog trainer and her sidekick and mentor dog, Buddy. There are six novels and four holiday novellas out in that series, which is set in north central Florida. A seventh novel is planned for late 2020/early 2021.

To read and see more about Kassandra and her books, please go to https://kassandralamb.com. Be sure to sign up for the news-letter there to get a heads up about new releases, plus special offers and bonuses for subscribers.

Kass's e-mail is lambkassandra3@gmail.com and she loves hearing from readers! She's also on Facebook, Goodreads, and Bookbub, and she hangs out some on Twitter @KassandraLamb. She blogs about psychological topics and other random things at https://misteriopress.com.

Kassandra also writes romantic suspense under the pen name of Jessica Dale (https://darkardorpublications.com/).

PLEASE CHECK OUT THESE OTHER GREAT *MISTERIO PRESS* SERIES:

Karma's A Bitch: Pet Psychic Mysteries
by Shannon Esposito

Multiple Motives: Kate Huntington Mysteries
by Kassandra Lamb

The Metaphysical Detective: Riga Hayworth Paranormal Mysteries
by Kirsten Weiss

Dangerous and Unseemly: Concordia Wells Historical Mysteries
by K.B. Owen

Murder, Honey: Carol Sabala Mysteries
by Vinnie Hansen

Buried in the Dark: Frankie O'Farrell Mysteries
by Shannon Esposito

To Kill A Labrador: Marcia Banks and Buddy Cozy Mysteries
by Kassandra Lamb

Lethal Assumptions: C.o.P. on the Scene Mysteries
by Kassandra Lamb

Payback: Unintended Consequences Romantic Suspense
by Jessica Dale

Never Sleep: Chronicles of a Lady Detective Historical Mysteries
by K.B. Owen

Bound: Witches of Doyle Cozy Mysteries
by Kirsten Weiss

At Wits' End Cozy Mysteries
by Kirsten Weiss

Steeped In Murder: Tea and Tarot Mysteries
by Kirsten Weiss

Steam and Sensibility: Sensibility Grey Steampunk Mysteries
by Kirsten Weiss

Big Shot: The Big Murder Mysteries
by Kirsten Weiss

The Perfectly Proper Paranormal Museum Mysteries
by Kirsten Weiss

**Plus even more great mysteries/thrillers at
https://misteriopress.com/bookstore/**

www.ingramcontent.com/pod-product-compliance
Lightning Source LLC
Chambersburg PA
CBHW020134180626
46810CB00004B/1554